The Journey of Water

KATHERINE DAVIES

Published by Spring Publishing, 2023

Cambridge, UK

ISBN 978-1-7391840-3-2

To Alex and Jean

1

Under whispering rain, the old capital stretched out its veins to the sky. Centuries of toil lay beneath the stone and towers. London, a refuge for which millions had risked drowning to reach, no longer held the attention of Elena Lees. She stood alone at the giant sliding door, watching pearls of water forming on the glass.

The wall-to-wall view of the city dominated the apartment. Facing north from the south bank of the Thames, you could see much of central London and a broad sweep beyond. It was a world away from the usual digs for London nurses. Elena's former 'place to sleep' was a room in a share house noteworthy for the pervasive smell of car fumes and takeaway.

At 37, with few possessions and a long way from home, Elena was, to anyone else she knew, most fortunate — her liaison with a wealthy trader the grand finale of a series of attempts to find enduring love. But fortunate she did not feel. She had her easy days. Thanks to years in nursing, and its many routines, she kept it together and largely concealed her true state to almost everybody, including herself. Her boyfriend was absent.

Born accomplished, Baxter Wyle enjoyed a lion's reputation in the financial markets, chiefly in his domain — complex strategies such as the 'jelly roll' and the 'straddle'. His stripe of bank eschewed empathic types like Elena, other than when their presence was required for a poignant perfidy of philanthropic marketing. But three years ago, knocked sideways by a huge trading loss, Baxter had drunk so much he nearly died, and he fell for the attentive Aussie gal in the Emergency Department of St Antony's Hospital. Why *she* fell for a monosyllabic banker soaked in urine remained a mystery.

For Baxter, bankers of his ilk would typically date a younger woman. Perhaps she offered 'the night-nurse package for the time-poor', she pondered later, as their relationship cooled, and they became the strangers they had always been.

But at the outset, as soon as the patient could walk and pee, Elena and Baxter became an item, or rather, Baxter and Elle. With their long working hours, dating proved a challenge logistically, and they were soon living together. It was the practical choice.

The first and last visit to Elle's place was brief. There was nowhere to park his car. Inside, he stood stiffly, unresponsive, facing the stains on the wallpaper. She wanted him to visit her bedroom where she had spent some time the night before washing and furnishing with plants and pictures, reordering her things to make a little space in the cupboard and empty a drawer. She was quite pleased with the result, and to the delight of her housemates, she kept going, tackling the communal bathroom and the kitchen. She was 'on a roll'.

Baxter, however, did not move his impeccable shoes until a zing emanated from his trouser pocket. As he walked out the crooked door, she saw his hand flick away as if to cast off a side of life he wanted nothing to do with. All at once, she felt mortified, sad, and glad she had covered the large stain on the living room sofa with a throw. She understood his reaction and followed in his wake. She cursed the front door as she lifted it to engage the lock. She did not notice the shadow in her heart. She was relieved to escape the dump where she lived and the hordes of traffic passing its door. She was excited to find the giant fishbowl had become her new home.

A glass dining table sat on the middle landing of a glass stairwell directly overlooking the metropolis. Invitees were checked for food allergies and a fear of heights after one lost more than her appetite over a splayed salmon from the north Atlantic. At first glance, the idea of the setting in the sky was impressive, but by the end of the first course, the view became like an extra guest groomed to draw one's attention but with little to say.

The groomed lobby looked more like a new hotel, with doors that swished and a concierge. After freeing herself from a crowded smelly bus, she would stroll through the tall leafy corridor and ascend to the 20th floor and the smooth clean lines of her new life. But even in the early heady days, and the rolls on the platinum shag, somewhere buried within her had felt ready to check out the next day. It was not long before her favorite place became the windowless bathroom.

She followed a tiny stream across the glass, down to the smooth planks of polished floor. Her feet were inches from the balcony. In the darkest of times, she could not stand on this spot, so close to the sliding door and the city below. Suicidal thoughts were only thoughts, but they had lingered like an undertow of dread. Despite her training, she had kept them to herself. But remarkably, at this very same spot, after a horrendous shift at work, the morbid ruminations came to an abrupt end. It was to be one of many strange experiences unaccounted for in her biology textbooks. At the time, it seemed to Elena, as if a surge of energy, both within and beyond herself, was pushing her back from entering the balcony; a defiant, life-affirming force that was as real as standing in the surf and being hit by a wave. The moment shocked her to the extent that she began forthwith to take deliberate steps to unmoor her melancholy. She was today, nowhere near nor perhaps ever would be completely resilient, but she was not made of granite and strides had been made. A consequence of this process was her current and unusual plan to escape the present circumstances of her life (whilst still living).

Baxi had never known nor noticed his girlfriend's state, or if he ever did, its severity did not register. She was having a bad day which would never come close to the shit he had to deal with on a daily basis. Baxter lived in another world, which for many of its inhabitants was the center of all that really mattered, and where he enjoyed some measure of power and status, where he felt in control. Everything in his realm had a price, and the long game was to do whatever you desired, with time you never had.

Elena pulled open the heavy door without trepidation. Holding the balcony rail, she surveyed the scene, enjoying the soft drops of rain on her face. She did not, as in earlier times, take in the sweep of history nor look for St Paul's or The Shard. Her attention was drawn to the parks and patches of green and the river. At street level, near the tower, Elena spotted school children rushing into a playground. At once, she remembered the sensation, running with her brother to the ocean, crashing through waves. Life in the sun. First sight of the sea.

"I see the sea and the sea sees me!" Elena and Freddie, her brother, would cry after stretching their necks in a stinking hot car vying to be the first to spot the Pacific. The interminable wait to find a place to park, to mark territory on the sand, to help carry and not drop all the bits and bobs, to be smeared with sticky sun cream, was all bearable only, because it would soon end in a triumphant splash and an endless day playing in and out of the surf.

Cheerful as a young child in Australia, open and friendly, here, perched high above one of human history's great cities, she had thought to end her life. It was the other end of what she imagined her future to be when as a child, after bedtime, she would lie on the cool grass in the back yard and share her dreams with the moon.

She re-entered the apartment, scanning the pristine steel and glass salon, the untouched books, the absence of memories. In a blink of a passing thought, she noticed that the water on her cheeks felt more real than the life she inhabited. She checked the sheen of the center table for imperfections. Baxter cared about such things but now it was just a habit. She felt the contents of her coat pockets and left for the river.

The direct route ran alongside commuter traffic, narrowing under a vast railway bridge. As she entered the dark underpass, a speeding car wheeled into the gutter right by her side and back onto the roadway. "Get a life!" she blurted out in fury as she pulled away from the pavement's edge and hugged the tunnel wall. The mild manners of the locals vanished with the light. She watched drivers careen and maneuver frantically to be first where first was meaningless.

The tunnel opened to a pedestrian junction. A large crowd crossed her path. She heard languages from around the world but knew they were locals, dressed as they were for the office and moving at speed. She slipped through the throng and over a six-lane-road before the lights changed. Leaving the street, she cut through a maze of apartment towers, head down, accustomed to the blasts of wind. At first glimpse of the Thames, she eased her pace. When the last wall ended in an arctic breeze, she tightened her coat, pausing on the concrete bank. The tide was high. The flowing water was all she could see within the frame of her hood and she spoke to it.

Thank you, old friend. So many times, you have been there for me.

Her shoulders dropped and she walked on. The swollen river rolled alongside, its mercurial surface shifting under the moving and enormous bank of cloud. Tourists and workers and the sprawling Thames flowed in lost time. Elena tried to calm her mind but to dwell on her thoughts only magnified the din, and the clamor and drone of the city crawled up her neck. She stopped trying.

In her mind's eye, on a crowded stage in lights, a pumping heart appeared, performing its biological routine. A band played, not entirely together or in tune. She recognized the tired faces — nurses, doctors, cleaners from her ward — and behind them, a choir of sorts, absorbed in song, swaying to the rhythm, soon outpaced by the beating of Elena's own heart. The choristers were all patients she had come to know who had come to die at the hospital. She heard the flow of water running underneath and the rocking of a wooden chair, on a porch, the sound of birdsong and the low humming of a tune. It was Beth, her Aunt Bethany who had recently passed, at her leafy home in Sydney. A book on her lap, the smell of pine, her questions.

"Joysie!" she cried, arms outstretched, standing in a garden riot. Her aunt had always called her Joy, or some variation, even the day after Elena's Mum — Beth's sister — had been committed to hospital. Elena had just turned 14.

"Ooh, you smell like gardenias," she said, hugging her niece, overdue for a shower.

"Oh, Aunty."

Beth held her niece close until she started to pull away.

"She'll be okay, my darling. I met the doctor, nurses, good people. I know the doctor in charge. She just needs some rest."

Rest, Elena thought. Her mother needed the world to stop. But her aunt was a therapist. She would understand her mother's condition and know the standard of care. If Elena herself, at 14, tried to comprehend her mother's illness, she was not just lost. Curled in her bed, the world would morph into cliffs of shadow. When her mother became manic, or caustic, people would say, 'just remember, she's ill', as if that was enough. The day before, she had heard it all, the desperate pleas with the police, the wild hollering for help, the clunk of the car door. She had heard it all, so clearly, despite her tears and her hands pressed hard against her ears as she sat crouched in the dirt by the side of the house. A few days later though, Elena was back, at the end of her aunt's garden by the Wollemi pine, sitting on the grass in the shade, shuddering, digging her army boots into the soil.

It was a summer's day, where the sun crushes the soft light of dawn like a tank. On a sofa on the veranda, Beth sat quietly, opening and closing a book. Eventually, her niece lay back, looking at the sky, and Beth made iced tea. They sat together. Elena pulled off her sweaty boots and hugged her knees. After a silence, Beth talked about the birds around her home, their calls and patterns, comings and goings.

"I wonder," she said, "is the kookaburra bettered in nature as the quintessential alarm clock. And at day's end, the colors! The colors offering, loved or lost — *my* concerns neither here nor there — the forever sky, the blooms, the rainbow lorikeets."

Elena struggled to listen. She looked at her aunt speaking.

"How, Aunty—," she said, clearing her throat. "What can I do, to stop the magpies diving at me?"

"Sorry, darling?"

"The magpies attack me, by the station, and here again, another crow. They're everywhere."

"Can you show me?"

"Look, there, there, on the gum," Elena said, darting her hand.

"That's a raven," her aunt replied, putting down her glass and sitting closer.

"A raven?"

"Magpies defend a nest," Beth said. "Don't walk the same way. Keep your distance from where they're nesting. As for crows… Let's see, what else can you spot?"

Elena looked at the treetops, barely moving her neck.

"Nothing."

Beth put her arm around her and pointed out a flush of lorikeets gossiping in the banksia, and a sulfur-crested cockatoo looking their way from a branch in the neighbor's yard.

"One day, my darling", she said, holding Elena close, "you will feel better, and you'll see and hear and feel all the birds, all the life, and there, right there, you will see your mother, very well, smiling, and love, so much love, pouring to you, from her open heart."

Elena looked down the length of the Thames and followed the winding in her mind through Greenwich and Gravesend out to the North Sea. The boats to Europe. The Europe of her mother's dreaming. A long way from kookaburras and surf. Her mother's sister had had the chance. On rare occasions, Aunty Beth shared with teenage Elena glimpses of her travels abroad, such as tumbling down the pistes of Obergurgl, and the time she gave her blood for money to pay for a flight to Beirut. Her eyes would shine in the telling. Years would fall from her face. But there was much she would not say, like *what happened in Beirut,* and her loves and loss, and what might have troubled her. Her choice of music, Angolan semba to Indian ragas, depended on her mood, and she would sometimes read aloud from one of her favorite books — The Oxford Dictionary of English Etymology, the works of Jung, or the comedies of P.G. Wodehouse. But to her niece, she revealed little of anything personal, even when Elena was older and had left Australia. They would speak on the phone, with more than 10,000 miles between them. While her aunt's past was a mystery, her present was not. In Elena's company, her aunt gave her time, entirely. She was never somewhere else. When they were together, time ceased to matter at all.

It was her aunt who had stepped into the void when her mother first lost her way.

Ahead, the river path was blocked. But Elena wasn't ready to turn back. She followed a detour around a construction site. When she returned alongside, the Thames was now a shade of black, reflecting the clouds above. More excited than concerned, the scene reminded her of home, where violent storms would sweep in and flash and streak and shake all the life, and leave behind a pristine air where for a moment, everything could begin again. And there it goes!

A hat flew past in an icy gust. She scooped up the worn flat cap, her fingers touching the silk lining. An older man repeated muffled thanks through the wrap of a thick scarf and shuffled away. She carried on, wiping water from her eyes, ignoring the spitting sky, pushing into the north wind, reaching back for the feel of Aunty Beth's bony embrace, her dusky perfume, their moments together from armchairs, trying and failing yet trying to interpret the world.

She rolled her shoulders. Rain had emptied the walkway. She stepped into a tiny café close enough to the water's edge to feel like a boat and ordered coffee. She pulled a stool to the best vantage point and removed her dripping coat. She could smell fried eggs and disinfectant. A tidy man in a one-button suit sat alone looking at documents, his finger running rapidly down each page. A phone vibrated and he was gone, subsumed in the black umbrellas on the bridge. She wondered if he was an estate agent, a civil servant, or a spy. The intelligence agencies were nearby. "Too much television!" she heard her mother say. The buzz from his mobile was loud, more like the old pagers her father used to wear. What was it, what was it *Dad* used to say. She searched in vain for a line from her father. The hazy eyes of elsewhere. To her, he was the sound of an empty room, a car pulling away, a pulsing pager – a device to which all responsibility was assigned.

No, that's unfair, she thought. His father, my father, our father.

She savored the aroma of her latte before taking a sip. Rain splattered the window. Across the road, two young women ran laughing into a former church beneath a bell tower from the 12th century. Now a museum, and Elena's favorite café for lunch, she knew Londoners had been praying at the spot since before the Normans. They had much to pray about back then, when a maze of filthy narrow streets was home, and illness, fire or plague a constant threat. The Anglican creed was aboard the first convict ships to Australia, and the tentacles of the Vatican were not far behind. It was a convict priest who delivered Sydney's first Catholic mass. Near Elena's childhood home, the local catholic school and church loomed large.

Sundays on a church pew, squeezed between fleshy women in freshly ironed dress. The parishioners waving away flies, flapping pages, lost in dreams. Hot cars, trapped children sniping, faces to the window, desperate to get out and join the trees. So many trees for a city, the size of Sydney, though the family home sat near its edges, where the footpath turned to bush.

Never wanting to leave the beach.

Never wanting to leave Rosa's side, the lady from Madrid who for years, came from the church, once a week, to help with the house, and held her close so many times, folded in her heart. What was it about a fleshy hug from Rosa? Was it that she demanded nothing, nothing at all, or that she was so grounded and *all there.* She wasn't thinking of other things. Her eyes would confirm it, though you needed none — a smile clean from the heart. Oh my, Elena thought, the many souls in this world who survive to adulthood without ever feeling this kind of love. Nothing to do or be or earn. It just is.

Rosa said so little and died so young, sending swallows to the sky. In Rosa's last days, the quiet nurse who cared for her inspired a trembling Ellie — not the only visitor who struggled to find something to say. Silences long and loud were no gift to the dying. But the nurse was never far, and with touch, a press on the shoulder, a few quiet words, Rosa's fear would drop away. The nurse might have been doing her job, and well, but Elena remembered what she saw as a manifestation of love the Greeks would call 'agape'.

Elena gazed through the café window at a ferry drifting past with an empty deck. The boat's wash unfurled silver fans across the water. The existence of universal love made sense to her, despite the disturbing and mounting evidence to the contrary, for herself and the whole sorry state of things — the horror stories of patients, the relentless news, dying forests and oceans, great fires and flood, the insanity of war, her own travels for work in harrowing outposts of humanity, a long way from sidewalks and hospitals. She had seen an underlying love in everyone she knew, and could remember knowing, sometimes buried beneath layers of rock. It felt utterly real and at the same time, unknown. For too long, it seemed to her, too many had played a part in the destruction of what was possible, often unwittingly. But this line of thought was hard to digest and left her feeling weak.

She caught her reflection and looked away, rubbing a rash on her arm. She had made progress but felt a long way from clear water herself. She'd been so lost, and reckless. Worrying about her job, and what others thought, she had not sought the help available to her at work when she needed it most, attempting to claw her own way back from depression. In the end, she drew support from a good number of people thanks to those who provided sound therapeutic advice online and had authored the books she consumed on mindfulness, sleep, outdoor exercise, the power of gratitude and forgiveness, and the deep intelligence in our bodies. There was the patient chi kung teacher, walks with friends, the kindness of strangers, and the journalists of the World Service in the middle of the night. Her guitar. And where would she be without a recourse to nature — the local park or the river or a moment in the garden at the hospital? She was now much better than she was, but to feel 'joy?' *Joy?* She was glad her aunt could not see her now. Weighed down by all of it, all of her life as she lived it, 'clarity' and 'ease' were dreams that eluded her, but she knew, she knew the next step. As crazy as the idea sounded, she felt its truth in the depth and fiber of her being.

She zipped up her coat and returned to the wet street, hit by a wall of fresh, cool air. She zigzagged through a crowd of tourists milling by a coach and taking pictures of the Palace of Westminster. The rain had stopped, and the great city swarmed again, but the one thing that filled her with energy was the thought of leaving. It would not be long now.

In the quest for calm and clarity, Elena had realized her body had its own language, and it had been waiting a long time to speak. The loudest message was strong and clear. She needed to get up and *go!* to leave the city, on foot, *to walk out*, and not to stop. To walk away from everything she knew, and just keep walking. To explore, to be in and with the forests and streams, to slip past her mind and to hear, in all their reaches, the birds and creatures, and feel the moss and sense all the life, to hike until her legs ached, to shake the stones out of her shoes, to drip with sweat, to scramble the heights and call all the soaring birds. She smiled at the flow of the river and felt a stretching in her heart.

2

It had been so easy. Baxter was away, travelling for work. Her boss was on holiday. St Antony's HR clerk handed her a simple form to give notice, barely looking away from her screen. Elena sat down by the desk, a few feet away and scanned the page. She did not like to lie and there was no need. There was no 'reason for leaving' sought. She paused before signing.

At the end of the corridor, on a row of unbreakable plastic chairs, a queue of patients waited for x-rays. A heaving man coughed into a paper towel. A woman held a stroller hung with shopping bags. Out the side drooped the leg of a young child. Elena's pen rolled off the clipboard onto the floor. Retrieving it without touching the floor, she noticed the upturned ring on her finger. She gently slid the silver band. The top half was shaped like a dolphin, or a drop of water, or a tear, or something else. Her mother had always been vague and playful about it, turning her gift into a question, turning everything into a question. Elena wondered what she would think, right now, about her plans, that is, her mum on a good day.

In the kitchen of her childhood, Elena saw her mother standing at the bench, looking up from a task, bright eyes alert and smiling, an easy breeze through the blind. Elena, imagining, sat at the table and spoke to her mother.

Patients, Mum, patients recover, die, stay the same. You do your job. Every day. My day starts when I slip on my uniform. I enter the logic and routines and what I've always done. But Mummy, on that day of last days, I was so low. A patient had died. It wasn't like it was the first time, preparing a corpse, you know, for a family. Sudden cardiac arrest, untreated myopathy. Time of death: 9:32. But it wasn't another cadaver. Brushed her dyed hair. It was sticky. Couldn't control my arm or stop the shake. I gripped the bed rail with one hand and with the other, I carefully wiped her pale face. Her lips were hard. Rigor mortis had reached her neck. That pearly scarf fell to the floor. Moments beneath the bed, out of sight, they saved me. Same slim nose, same high cheekbones, wrists so thin you thought they'd break. Yes Mum, she looked like you.

At the end of that endless shift, in the meds office, shoving boxes of Prozac in my bag, how edgeless I was, how raw, how everyone and everything seemed so cold and distant, so very alone, until I reached the door, the door back to the world. As if someone had flicked a switch on the passing of time. I had the chance to pause. I could feel a resistance near my hand, between my hand and the handle. And right then, from the other side of the door, I heard the sound of little bells! *Little bells.* A volunteer was pushing the book trolley through the ward, ringing the toy to let patients know the nearness of a good book. I stopped — thanking all that is good — turned around, and put all the meds back, every one. In my heart, I was on my knees.

With sudden ease, Elena looked down at the form and signed her name and herself to an unknown future.

Hana, Elena's closest colleague and boss, was due back from leave a week later. She agreed to meet the first morning, at Fatima's, an American-diner-style café popular with staff right next to the hospital entrance. She would be busy, short of time, perhaps late, but key for Elena was that it was Hana's first day back, and their meet-up was outside the ward.

Red booths lined the wall. Elena sipped her coffee and rested back against the vinyl. It had been a strange week. Her nursing colleagues — whether curious, alarmed, or bored — slipped in a question at every turn, the answers to which she barely knew herself. It was customary to bid farewell over a drink at the 'local' and she would repeat on the ward that by then, she would have answers. She looked around Fatima's where the tea was good and cheap. This would be her 'local' and her last shift would be through the night. The stragglers would fit in one booth. And no one would hassle her after graveyard.

An older couple sat together silently in the opposite corner, looking out the window, waiting. Nearly empty, the café was oddly noisy, outside and in. The vents of the hospital, the revving engine of a passing truck, the clinking of plates, the sound of talk radio. On the wall, a young Aretha Franklin was striding through a London park, in long boots and a paisley dress, her arms raised in the air. Beneath her, a student munching toast, hunched over a fat textbook, tapped the table repeatedly with a pencil.

A medic rushed through the doors and ordered coffee to go. Behind her strode a blood courier. Red thermal bag slung across his padded jacket, he spoke in a rapid murmur on an invisible phone. Outside, a throng of people emptied from a bus and among them was not one single dawdler nor new arrival to London pausing to check directions. They all headed straight to St Antony's, queueing to enter the revolving doors of their working day. Everyone was in the middle of something, in action, and Elena felt detached from it all. The doctor waiting for her coffee was jumpy, checking her phone. Elena looked for messages on hers. She scratched her skin. The underside of her forearm was inflamed.

Baxter was in South America. He was either working, travelling for work, or dreaming about work. Her role, somewhat down the food chain, now appeared to be functional, services she suspected would soon be supplied by another if she wasn't already in place. The early days of languishing, random jaunts and grass stains had long expired. She shifted on her seat, glancing at the couple at the far end. She tried and failed to pinpoint the missteps.

Easy to remember Dorset, their first weekend away, lying on a blanket by the coast, sharing everything. The salty breeze and sweaty skin and squawking birds. Moments furled away unsullied in her mind.

"What do you dream?" Baxter had asked her, facing the sky.

"That mum gets better," she said, stroking the side of his chest. "And patients notice, what's happening in their lives, before it makes them so sick, they end up in hospital."

"You want an empty hospital? What would you do?"

She laughed, nervously. "I don't know," she said, lying on her back. "I've always been a nurse. I was a dreamer, in my backyard, at home, as a kid, I used to dream. I must have had the chore of watering the garden. I was out there a lot."

"What did you want to be back then?"

"You'll laugh."

"Try me."

"For a while, I thought I'd be a nun!"

"A nun!"

"Yes, some of my teachers at school were nuns. I didn't tell anyone, it was just a secret I had for a little while, until I thought through the lifestyle. Kind of rules out fornicating on cliff tops."

Sniggering, Baxter rolled on his side to face her as a seagull flapped about behind him.

"I also dreamt of being an artist," Elena continued, "musician, activist. I didn't have a clue really. What about you? What did you dream as a boy?"

He turned and punched his fist towards the sky arching his ribs.

"I wanted to be Mick Jagger."

Elena laughed.

"Another time," he said, "I made a lab in the garden shed and asked for equipment as gifts for Christmas. Fantastic. Used to love making things blow up. And making things, pulling things apart, putting them back together."

"Did you get hurt?"

"No. The shed is still standing, though needs repair. My family lived next to a forest."

"Oh, how beautiful! I know what that's like! You must've had many adventures."

"Yes, someone else lives there now, but soon, soon I will buy it back."

And he did.

When in town, Baxter's days and evenings were spent in the City of London, the financial district. From what she had learned from him, and many of her patients in its orbit, there were nameless men, and they were usually men, leaning on everyone beneath them to do whatever it took to beat an impossible annual target, pitched higher year on year. Nobody was stopping them. Broken families and whole countries lay in their wake.

Outside the diner, Elena heard a rumble in the traffic, a machine that belonged on a racetrack. She spotted it trying to switch lanes, hemmed in, held back, pent up having to tolerate what, other humans? Living things? The absence and conditional love of their parents? Baxter owned something similar with which he would constantly challenge or ignore the speed limit. The last time she was a passenger they were late for a Sunday lunch, winding through holiday traffic on the M25, listening to The Stranglers, passing family cars stuffed with bags, parasols, canoes, dogs. Baxter cruised on by, tapping gears with his fingers. There were no 'bags' in the vehicle. No fingerprints on the window. The way he liked the sheen of his dreams.

Oh Ellie. The boats I have chosen to board. Trying to be calm I was, to sit still on the leather seat, to stop myself from gripping the ergonomic armrests, pleading silently for the journey to be over. Only the music changed. What was it? Something smooth and breathy. The latest incarnation of the sexy supplicant. I saw myself merging with the leather, thinking 'I wasn't beautiful enough', and dismissing the thought with the thought — *how low can I go?*

Ah yes, I sat there, feeling compassion for the multi-millionaire singer, wondering if there was a nutcase somewhere trying to invent a car that could give you an orgasm, and realizing, they already existed. We passed a boy, glued to his car window, excited, staring at us, staring at a story. He could not see the trap, the man next to me, his thin smile, sewn skin, workaholic life, the images rolling in my mind of everyone Baxter had ever loved and never saw, and every life experience he'd missed, as he paid for the swagger in time.

And whose trap was it? Who did *I love* that I never saw.

Elena gulped her coffee and tilted forward, shifting in her seat. She looked on the inside of her arm and pressed her hand against the itching rash. She sat on her hands and looked outside.

My exodus— oh, that's a good one. My *exodus* begins

before he gets back, thanking all that is good.

She looked at her phone, scrolling through pages.

Nah, nothing. Not a single call or message from wherever he is. Maybe I should leave him a farewell letter. Ha! I wonder, yes, I will leave it on the side table. How long will it take for him to notice?

A message from Fran.

Elena had booked her friends, Franny, Della and Joe, for dinner at a new curry house. It would be her last Friday night in London, at least for the foreseeable future. Best that way, she thought.

The coffee machine had begun to whir incessantly, whittling down a queue of caffeine addicts that had formed at the till.

No sign of Hana.

She pulled out her notebook and skimmed through her 'to dos' which were more of a list of questions. Planning to walk out of London, and keep on walking, with no specific destination in mind, was not straightforward.

There were four weeks to go. In a month, it would be Spring. There were practical questions. Where to stay? Camp solo? Carry a tent and sleeping bag, walk long distances with a heavy load? Jump on trains to scenic places? Stay at BnBs? She had savings and Beth had left her money, but she'd need to take care, not knowing when her next paycheck would be. As for the route, should she use walking paths and enjoy nature – without shelter or a ready supply of provisions – or should she follow roads through more settled areas?

"More coffee?"

A dress the color of bluebirds. She never wore dresses.

"Thank you, Fatima. Love the color!"

"Thank *you.*" The café owner-manager asked a question she had posed before. Elena thought, wrongly, she asked the same to all her regulars. "So, how's the circus?"

Elena laughed, stiffly. She caught Fatima's penetrating look and twisted her inflamed arm out of sight.

"We've some rhinos, blind rhinos," Elena said, "wandering the wards, but the clowns are well-behaved."

Fatima grinned, revealing again, her love of all things American. Her teeth were bleached white. She kept talking as she wiped the next table. The student had left a wide splatter of crumbs.

"Haven't seen you in a while," she said. "Taking care, Sister Lee?"

"Yes, yes, and you?"

She ignored the question, methodically wiping the edge of the table.

"It's rough out there?" she asked finally, glancing up.

Elena's neck tightened.

Fatima binned the crumbs and returned to wipe down the seat. Elena wanted to utter some noise, but the question was too close.

"You should take good care, my friend," she said.

"Thank you, Fatima."

At the counter, she stopped and turned around, looking at the picture of Aretha. She faced her customer.

"Glory," she said. "You look after yourself Sr Lee, and come in here, one day, and look like that (pointing at

Aretha), when you *feeel* like that? Breakfast is on me." She tapped her chest.

Elena laughed and spluttered.

"Oh, you're awesome. Deal!"

Fatima smiled and left for the kitchen.

"Thank you!" Elena called after her, loudly, for a café in England. "You're an angel!"

Fatima walked back out beaming, carrying a tray towards the couple.

"How will you know?" Elena called out again.

Fatima huffed.

"How do you know when a woman can sing and a man can dance?"

"Aww."

The flash of blue disappeared again. Elena looked up at Aretha and sagged in her seat. It would be a long road.

Outside, the traffic crawled towards the inner city. She looked for the faces of drivers but they were too far away. She floated in her mind up to the sky and watched the stream from high above and all the traffic converging on central London. She too had been on the bus that morning. She was of it; she was part of it all. Shunting towards the rest of our lives.

Too long. Is it just too long, living *here*? Always on. The constant noise and attack on the senses. A giant field of distortion. No relief. No sanctuary. Where is the girl I was, the young woman who looked at the world as it was and rolled up her sleeves.

She felt the urge to lie down.

Is it just overwork, the never-ending shifts dragging from one to the next? I feel you laden heart. Whatever it is, drawn I am, drawn to quiet forests, clean rivers and streams, hiking in mountains. And alone.

Alone. A woman alone. Niggling they did, the questions. There we were, young girls, eager to learn, swiftly learning to accept the unacceptable. The cradle of fear. For us and against us and created by none of us.

She looked up at the Queen of Soul.

I'll be safe enough. This creep of invisibility around men. Pah! Damn handy if you're hitting the road. To think, I had wanted to claim my first facial lines as marks of a life lived, attracting respect. What planet was that. Not in inner London. Not what I've seen, paying attention, clinical attention, after hours, to the behavior of men my age. She caressed the newfound creases on her forehead. They will help keep me safe. And Europe really doesn't do wilderness. There are people everywhere.

A colleague from radiology she vaguely knew walked towards the entrance to Fatima's. Elena looked down at her notebook, flicking through pages. She stopped at the training record.

After reading up on long distance, she had started to walk to and from work - a total distance of nearly 12 kilometers or 8 miles. No more elevators. According to the advice, she needed 'legs', though she expected walking for 10-hour-plus-shifts most of her adult life was a good place to start. Requirements included wicking fabrics, layers, worn-in walking shoes and cotton socks.

And then there were the fears, in the faces of colleagues, concerned as to what might have led her to want to walk alone and without a plan. She could not understand why she felt more excited than anxious, why she was drawn to silence, solitude, connecting with the natural world. She just knew she *had to* with every sinew in her body.

"Elena!"

An older woman in scrubs carrying a bag of groceries stood in front of her booth.

"Day one and I get your news."

"Hana! Sorry! It's *great* to see you! How was your break?"

"Leaving the fourth floor? Really? What on earth for?"

They both smiled and she took a seat.

Elena's hands started to tremble. Hana had come out of nowhere. She hadn't seen her enter. After all the waiting, she wasn't ready. As soon as she saw her knowing eyes, a rush of memories came all at once. The care of patients on the edge of life. The unexpected farce. The tap-dancing fundraiser. The secret hunt for the missing prosthetic. The day they hid little Brody. Elena held the trembling boy behind a storage trolley, while Hana sent his rampaging father up the wrong stairwell and locked down the floor. They thought they had witnessed the many forms of grief until Brody's father lost his wife.

Elena wiped away the start of tears. She knew the swelling in her heart was love, a comradely love. The pair had worked together closely and often under pressure. Both were known for good judgement under stress, but they also shared the knack of finding levity in the dark, cheering up the ordinarily inconsolable, or each other after an exhausting shift.

"I can't talk you out of it?" Hana said. "Can you let me try?"

A young man emerged from the kitchen and took Hana's order for coffee, takeaway. It was the same student who had sat in the adjacent booth munching toast.

"I haven't told any of the others…" Elena said.

"Yes, that's right. You can tell *me*. Between us." She leaned forward.

Elena looked away.

"I'm not, not 100 percent myself. I'm not so well."

Hana held Elena's hands. For a while they just sat together, still, silent, Elena with her eyes almost closed. Her boss sat back. "Sister," she said, "I know I have given you stick, too many times. You know, I didn't have any choice. All those patients you sat with in your way, listening, until I had to speed you along. And noticing what others would miss. And now, what have *I* missed? And what will the fourth floor be like when you're gone."

Elena half-smiled, scrunching her nose, shifting in her seat. She scratched her skin.

"Maybe… you'll win a Tim Tam."

Hana chortled. Nurses placed secret bets on the personal preferences of doctors. Success won an Australian chocolate biscuit. She looked straight at Elena.

"Is it Baxter?" she asked. "Are you safe?"

"Yes, nothing like that." Elena wiped her eyes. "I mean that was over, a while ago. He's rarely around and then, well, I think he just wants a nurse, with benefits."

Hana laughed, deep in her throat. She smiled broadly at Elena and glanced at her fob. "Well, you know you can move out anytime. I can get you a staffer."

"Thank you. It's more than that. I need to get away, to have a break, from all this."

"Ah, you Aussies... Too much fresh air and open spaces. Well, you know, as long as I run the 4th, you have a place here if you want to come back. It may not be the same role, but we can work out something."

"Thank you, Hana. You're so kind to me!"

Hana turned, looking for the waiter.

"How was your holiday?" Elena asked.

She swung back.

"Beautiful. Did absolutely nothing. My family has a cottage in the Welsh countryside. Where y'headin'?"

"Working on it."

"Good. Keep me posted. Sorry, got to go," Hana said, rising. "Take it easy girl. Need any less shifts let me know. Help with anything, let me know. I mean it."

Elena nodded with a smile. Only three years together and they had seen so much. Her foot started tapping.

3

The fourth floor at St Antony's was a warren of wards and corridors, waiting rooms and double doors. It was noisy. Alarms, rattling trolleys, ringing phones, the drone of vents, machinery and television, the buzz of fluorescent lights, the drag of metal curtain rings, the ebb and flow of chatter and rule at the nurses' station, all rolled on, to a greater or lesser degree, 24/7, perfumed with a whiff of formaldehyde.

But after giving notice, it was no longer the same place. Elena would soon be moving on, and to an open road. Shift after shift, in between attending to patients, training new staff, updating records, she would pull back, and notice where she was. During her now slower commute, she would have the chance to try to understand. She had left hospitals before, but this felt different. Pounding the city pavements from hospital to home, the questions kept coming.

Is it that I am older, more senior? Fifteen years now, or is it 16?

Is it time to give it all a rest?

Was this the world of my dreams? Is this what I wanted, the girl-me lying on the cool grass? Is this it?

Maybe my nursing days are truly coming to an end.

But what else could I do?

Maybe girl, the break will answer that.

What would I miss? *(laughing)*

Ah, there you go, memory slideshow, fresh and fading, hot and cold. Edited, again, and again, my mind's ever-diligent department of video production.

What are they *really*, yes, moments together, human, real, loving — though we never call it that. 'Colleagues'. We are more than that. Are they 'my people'? My tribe? There's elders and novices yes, a shared language, in-jokes, rituals, a code, a sense of purpose. There's no question, the importance of what we do, for a living, for a life. The closer I am to the door, the more respect I feel for what I am leaving.

As the last days wore on, Elena noticed too the qualities of a particular kind of exhaustion, unrelated to the miles she was clocking to and from work. A wave of fatigue would hit her under moments of stress, or when she noticed a patient needed care beyond the defined duties. It could at times be suffocating and she would need to find a moment's solitude and restore her focus.

At the same time, pursuits outside work brought a new and increasing joy. She sensed her whole body, and subconscious mind, were thrilled with her plans. More time each day was spent outdoors, preparing for her journey. Glancing up at slots of sky, she knew her vista would soon open wide. Walking through parks, breathing noticeably fresher air, she knew this would become her new normal. She marveled at her strengthening legs and the energy in her step and how she could now climb twenty floors without a pause. Her breathing would be labored and the last floors slow, but she didn't need to stop.

At a self-defense workshop in Krav Maga, she learned how relatively simple it was to disable an attacker. The knowledge gave her confidence. But the prospect of actually harming another was not the pleasure it seemed to be to the tired trio of scrub nurses who, laughing and shouting obscenities, thrilled to have the chance to pretend to poke out someone's eye or knee their groin.

For the walk to work, she kept to a route through local parks and minor roads. The commute became her makeshift laboratory. She tested various aspects of her expedition and kit, such as varying the load weight, different clothing, the consequences of wet weather, and the fabric of her knickers. Planning the trek out of London, she decided she would walk to the coast and on to France via roadways and settled areas, and then shift to walking paths later, once she was strong and confident solo and understood her daily limits. Elena had travelled alone before but had not done much hiking and never long-distance. She knew her friend Della, an experienced hiker, would interrogate her when they met for curry.

In the end, her friend was away, as explained in a call, on the day. It was London, Elena thought, remembering the times before. People not showing up or cancelling last minute was normal. At least she called.

"Before you go," Elena said, as her friend was about to hang up, "I'd best mention, I won't be around for a while. Taking a break. It was why I booked tonight."

"Lucky you! How long?"

"Not sure."

"What?! Have you left work?"

"Yes."

"Shit! When were you going to tell me?"

"Tonight."

"No! Finn, no. Don't touch, honey. Here, here. Is Baxter joining you?"

"No. We're... over."

Silence.

"Della?"

"I'm sorry, Elle. Knew things weren't well, but I didn't think, didn't know. I'm away now, tomorrow, with the kids, to Mum's. When do you leave?"

"Wednesday."

"Where you off to?"

"It's a long walk, to France, maybe further, not sure yet, will see how I go."

"Hang on, sorry? What? *Long* distance walking?"

"Yeah, walking out of London and keeping on going kinda thing. Though I may switch it up, take the train, it depends. I want to stay flexible. No pressure."

"I see. Alone?"

"Yes."

"Are you *insane?*"

"No."

"Bit young for a midlife crisis."

"Is that still a thing?"

"Crazy. How fit are you?"

"Pretty good. I've been walking 12 k every day, 6 out of 7, more or less, for the past four weeks."

"Oh, well. Wow. Why exactly didn't you call me? It would've been great to meet up!"

"Yeah. Sorry, Dell. I guess, I was worried you might talk me out of it."

"That makes sense... It's extreme, on your own, all that way."

"It's not easy to explain. Work's worn me down. The noise, the city... I can't think clearly anymore. It's all, need a long walk, be in nature."

"Fair enough, fair enough, girl. Hah! I think I'm jealous. Wouldn't mind joining you! Walking out the door. Won't have the chance this side of forever!"

4

The last Sunday in London, Elena squeezed all her belongings into a rental and drove to Wales, bound for Hana's family cottage in the hills near Porthmadog. Hers was the slowest car on the motorway. Unconcerned by the constant overtaking, she sang along to the tunes on the radio, both the ones she knew and the ones she didn't. A hangover had finally lifted and now and then, she would suddenly laugh. The night before last had been curry night.

Intuiting that Elena had not wanted to talk about her plans, nor her reasons for leaving, her friends, Franny and Joe, a long-time couple, had exhausted their news and switched to a novel drinking game — novel in that none of them had consumed reckless amounts of booze since university days. But given Elena's unusual and imminent departure, and the strange question it left in the air, it seemed, at the time, the appropriate thing to do. The 'new curry house' in Charing Cross Road was in fact, a pub with new grub, but the curry was delicious and spicy, inviting lavish lubrications. Joe, a solicitor, who dabbled in amateur theatre, had heard of the game 'Straight Face' from a barrister friend.

"Tell us more," said Elena.

"Okay, okay" he said, "it's as simple as fish."

"Fish?" said Franny. "Have you seen the sand art of the Japanese Puffer?"

"Right."

"Dolphins have rescued people," she continued, "lifting the injured to the surface so they can breathe."

"Wow, that's awesome," said Elena.

"Okay, okay," said Joe. "Fish are complex living creatures, unlike this game."

"Yes, love," Franny said, "of course, we need simple."

The couple shared a grimace.

"Love a game," said Elena. "Thank you, Joe."

"Right then," he continued. "Silly, just silly, nothing more than silly sentences, are written on strips of paper, by each participant, that anyone would struggle to read without a smile."

Both women smiled.

"Taking turns," he said, speaking succinctly, "players choose, from the overturned pile, one sentence at a time, reading aloud. If caught with the *slightest* smile or snigger, they must drink."

"Love it," said Elena, ignoring Franny's puzzled look. "Paper and pens!" Elena said, leaping up and heading towards the bar.

The trio were all keen to play, but there was just one

minor problem. It was a drinking game and none of them drank, not really. The obliging barman from the Urals by way of Imperial College found three small glasses and offered to deliver a fresh jug of beer if it ran low.

Ran low it soon did. Tipsy they soon were. Franny, a molecular biologist, with a passion for astronomy, had worried most she couldn't write anything remotely funny, but it turned out, after a few rounds, that actual humor was not required. Expressions of nonsense were the easiest and most successful. Elena landed on a form of questions that worked every time, even on herself.

"On Sundays, I rapidly recite a lurid limerick to my Great Aunt Savannah Schafernaker whilst clenching my left buttock and quivering my right — True or False?"

Franny found her mark with alliteration which became ruder as the night wore on.

"Mouldering Mary makes moping Michael muck mothering moose morbidly."

But on the glorious road to Porthmadog, Elena was remembering Joe, late in the night, leaping up and broadcasting his sentence to the now-loud crowded pub, standing on his chair. He was thrilled to have picked, by chance, his own sentence, which contained one of the longest words in the English language.

"Weeeeeeeee are the knights! who say - honorificabilitudinitatibus, five geese, and, a ham and cheese toastie! Thank you, thank you."

Applause from similarly plastered fellow patrons triggered a beaming smile and he emptied his glass. A few planks away, a man in a well-cut suit with a ripped shirt hanging out of his trousers, climbed slowly up his table to stand tottering on his chair, his friends laughing. He threw his arms in the air.

"We are…the knights…who say fffffffff - this went on for some time - ffffffff fee fai fo fumb, *I smell the blood of a drunken bum!*"

He fell back in his seat, his butt slamming the seat of the chair. The crowd roared its approval. And as the din dimmed, something shifted on its axis. It was as if the room had turned into the innards of a ship, and a charge was lit through the moldy-beer air. A large man by the window stood on his bench. He was every muscle struggled to find a place kind of large. He had a deep cavernous voice you couldn't ignore.

"We are the knights who say… Ka mate, ka mate."

"Ka ora' Ka ora'!" roared around the pub, from what must have been another dozen men. Elena could not remember but they seemed to be everywhere and huge. There was a deep visceral resonance to the chant, uttered in perfect unison. The crowd was stunned. Many of the punters had been so absorbed in their own waxings they hadn't noticed the arrival of an entire rugby team from the South Pacific.

"Ka mate, Ka mate," he repeated.

"Ka ora', Ka ora'!" came the great reply, like an invincible call, from centuries ago.

And then he sat back down and the pub returned to where it was. But no one else got up on their chair.

The night descended into a blur from there on in ending in Abingdon Street, with Joe losing a dare and mooning in front of what he thought was the House of Lords before the trio were shooed away by police. He had assumed that the 100-meter-high Victoria Tower was part of the Lords — the latter the subject of an unintelligible rant — but it was the home of the parliamentary archive.

Elena arrived at her destination in the Welsh countryside in darkness. It took some time, reversing with dipped lights across a country road, to find the right entrance. The stone cottage belonged to Hana's family. As she pulled opened the driveway gate, she could make out the outline of a house and chimney and a line of trees. She drove gingerly down a loose stone track around the back with a passing thought that the car might fall apart. The shed was exactly where it was meant to be. Standing and stretching on the grass, she filled herself with the scent of sleeping trees. A tick tick tick from beneath her car pulled her back. The key to the shed door worked easily. Once inside, she reached along the wall and found a switch, whooping out loud at the light.

The shed was half full of dusty boxes, bikes, children's pictures and gardening tools. Box by box, from the car to a corner of the shed, she arranged her things to take up as little space as possible. She placed a picture tube at the back, out of sight, and made room for her guitar, slowly slipping the hard case in place.

I'll be back, *my darling*, she said. As the words were uttered, she smelt fruit. Damn fruit. Strawberries. Summer. Baxter. The day before, she had sat in the corner of the old church café in Lambeth to write her farewell letter.

She stood back in the shed. The salty, nutty taste of his skin. My darling — a river of feeling, or none at all. How blind I was, naïve, lonely. Maybe back then, he really did mean it and cared for me. He did, surely? But he had signed up for another life, and allowed his time and true treasure to be swallowed whole. Everything else lost its value, including me. Funny I still bothered, right till the end, the way he liked things, rewriting the first draft. He never liked things messy. But it was an easy letter to write. He preferred 'matter-of-fact' and so it was.

> Dear Baxi
> I hope you had a good trip.
> By the time you read this, I will have left and be travelling abroad. I am sorry for not speaking to you in person. I needed badly to leave. And we have not really spoken, for a while.
> No doubt this note is of no great surprise. It is past time, I think you'd agree, we called where we are for what it is, and went our separate ways.
> Practically, I no longer work nor live in London, I deposited my next rent, retrieved my things, and arranged a redirection. In case you're in touch, by now my mates know, and know no more than this letter, as this business is ours. I send you my very best, and will hold our good memories for the pleasures they are.
> Elle

She walked outside and shook her thoughts away in the night air. The clouds had scattered. She gasped at the sight of the stars, absorbing their beauty, wondering how her life was changing in ways beyond her understanding. A rush of energy up her spine returned her to the mission. The last items to pull from the car were the heaviest, her medical library. They shouldn't be *this* heavy, she thought, reminded of her body's weakness above the navel and the online advice from hikers to cross-train. As she struggled with the weight, she made a mental note to add 'press-ups' to her routine. She would need to start at the level of a dresser.

She lugged the final book into place and took stock of her possessions. She had sold or given away the things she no longer needed. Given there was not much to start with, she was surprised when with the dispatch of each item, she felt a commensurate and delicious sense of letting go within her body. With the thought now of the imminent start of her adventure, she swiftly regained her zip. The natural world had aroused her senses, and thanks to Hana, another piece was falling into place.

Wednesday morning arrived. It was no ordinary Wednesday. From the moment she awoke in Baxter's flat, everything felt new, everything.

Elena rolled around on the huge mattress like a child, playing with the top sheet, and giving thanks to the God of beds. The hot shower was a tropical waterfall. At the sight of the laid-out walking clothes she paused, as if entering a monastery. She pulled on a t-shirt of Baxter's, opened the window, and stepped back. Every day now started with a brief session of chi kung. Today, and for the foreseeable future, there was no rush.

She stood still, breathing through her nose and out her mouth, taking care to balance the weight of her body evenly over her feet. She scanned her body and let go of tension. Once relaxed, as Sifu had taught, she 'smiled from the heart'. After a few minutes of stillness, she slowly stretched her arms above her head and commenced three techniques she could remember from the weekend's instruction. She loved the names — 'Lifting the Sky, Pushing Mountains and Carrying the Moon' — and how they made her feel after entering a 'chi kung state of mind' which was impossible to explain to anyone let alone herself, so she had given up trying. She yielded to the flow of chi and the peace of the present. The closing movement – blocking her ears whilst lightly tapping the back of the head – was called 'beating the heavenly drum'.

Calmly and methodically, she dressed in her new uniform of walking clothes, made the bed, left the letter and keys in place for Baxter, checked her rucksack, filled her water bottles, took the lift to the ground floor, and walked out the door.

5

A rude freshness filled the early morning air. The streets were quiet and empty. They belonged to Elena Lees. Her body filled with energy as she set off. She wanted to sing out loud.

Her stride was long, swift and even. She glanced at a laminated pocket list of street names. Her route out of the capital would take her towards Canterbury and the English Channel. Her senses awakened, she felt acutely aware of her surroundings. She passed the odd early riser pulling out shop wares, sweeping the littered street front.

London was largely asleep. Strangely to Elena, it seemed more alive, but she felt grateful for her direction out of town. Something told her she would never again call the capital home, nor any major city. She thought of the different areas where she had lived. They were not neighborhoods in the common understanding. Few people seemed to know each other nor stay for long. No one she had befriended in the early days still lived in the same place or even the same country.

The exhilaration of arriving for the first time. The blur of pubs and clubs, museums, galleries, world class artists routinely performing live. A wander down an inner-city street to find a long echo of history. The walls did speak with reminders that London was long a magnet for the brilliant and the persecuted. Stories were etched in the stone and monuments and fabric of the city.

She came to know and appreciate, in many Londoners, the instinct for freedom alongside a deeply ingrained respect for fairness and the law, apparent in the ebb and flow of city life. She fell in love with the diversity, learning about different cultures, histories, traditions, cuisines, in a living classroom. Entire streets and markets were seemingly lifted from another part of the world. *The music!* Dancing to live bands from Nigeria and Brazil, and on the back seats of minicabs after urging drivers with little English to turn up their favorites from home.

It took a while to adapt to the weather. The bitter cold of her first winter, running from one place to the next. Discovering thermal underwear and 'dressing in layers' and how, relatively speaking, London wasn't really that cold. Finding, after a chilly muddy walk, the delights of mulled wine in pubs with fireplaces. Getting through February with a visit to a sauna, a good coat, beanie and gloves, a few stiff drinks, and a hug or two. But the older memories were less clear, less reliable. The meaning, she thought, was the way the experience of living here expanded one's ways of seeing and one's understanding of the world.

She tried to imagine her life without London in it. It seemed calmer, kinder, more patient, less demanding, more loving perhaps, less stressful, but *smaller*, and smaller was the last thing her younger self could stand. She had been far too curious about the world. She would have hitchhiked on a spaceship. Would she ever be so curious again, in the same way? Ready, open, loving, fearless? Hmmm, she thought. I may just be too battered about for that. This thought made her laugh out loud as she saw herself walking solo out of London, to wherever. It wasn't as if she was riddled with fear.

In Greenwich Park, walking between heaving pink blossoms, she slowed to a stroll. An old tree with a massive twisted trunk and wild branches drew her attention. She rested against it and took in the tended gardens, the smell of grass, and thrilled at the thought of the nature to come. As she walked away, she stopped and turned around to where she had been leaning.

This was no ordinary tree. It was almost charismatic. There was drama and adventure in its convoluted trunk and asymmetrical arms. There were no straight lines about it. She walked the full circle around its base and without any arboreal expertise, examined its health. She felt an affection for what seemed like a living monument. A few meters away, a gardener watered a flower bed.

"Good morning," Elena said.

"Hello there," he said quietly.

"May I ask you, what kind of tree is this?"

"Sweet chestnut."

"Oh, thank-you."

"A seven-hundred-year-old sweet chestnut," he said, without the slightest change in expression.

"Wow! That's amazing! Thank you!"

He nodded slightly and turned away to water an adjacent bed.

Seven centuries! Sitting in that patch of grass. While the news delighted her, the conversation with another human — as illuminating as it was — broke the kind of spell she had felt, and the pull to move on became stronger than the urge to stay. Touching the bark, she whispered 'thank you'. As she left, glancing back, she tried to imagine life when it was a seedling, in medieval London. Perhaps she would have been standing outside London, in the countryside. For starters, she realized, she would have been dead. Life ordinarily ended at 29. She pictured entering London on foot, the cramped winding lanes, bustling market stalls, gossip and mead, town criers, fevers in the middle of the night, the nearness of death, sermons full of wrath. At the same time, she wondered, all the deeper things that truly matter to us now, mattered to us then? The city's population was only 80,000 souls. It was now more than 8 million.

The further out she walked, the more she appreciated how little of modern London she really knew. She looked for homes and often found in their place small featureless boxes of grey, glued to one another in long rows. Each doorway would open to another world, she thought, but from the outside, at first glance, it looked as if whole suburbs had been built heartlessly, from a distance, and at the least possible cost. She wondered if these fast suburbs were built in the ruins of a bombing raid, and with a desire to secure as many people as possible a place to call home. It was always a shock to learn that a building she was looking at, or living in, was once a crater from the Blitz. She walked on, and the streets felt unknown, and she saw the depth of her ignorance. This reflection lightened her step, as odd as that seemed, and oddness she did increasingly feel.

Underneath the steady rhythm of her gait, there crept an anxious sense of incredulity. It lingered throughout the day, through breakfast in a cheap and greasy, and out to the end of London, en route to Dover. She felt removed from her experience and couldn't pinpoint why. It was the last thing she expected. At one moment, she saw herself walking, from the sky overhead, this small slow-moving dot surrounded by tar, concrete and speeding objects. The more she dwelled on the sensation, the more alienated she felt, and a fear and numbness began to creep into her heart. But she was soon distracted by practical challenges.

She had noticed since leaving the city's edges, that in either direction, no one else was walking. Traffic was her companion and made the only noise she heard.

She followed her phone map's indications of a suitable walking path to Canterbury and found herself on the side of a highway, strewn with litter, with no space for pedestrians. On one side, right next to her, was a high metal fence, on the other, tarmac. Large trucks trundled by.

At first, frightened by the sudden hazard, she kept repeating out loud, with increasing volume "this is not a path!" She searched for a gap in the wire. She wanted to run but a slip might have sent her into the carriageway. Adding to the challenge were a distended bladder and lances of roadside nettle. Profanity became a helpful therapeutic, as was arguing with anonymous traffic, knowing she could not be heard, and, where she was walking, was probably illegal.

"Mootabelly shovel-headed kak jacker! Blagger off! Blaggahh!! So what, you are carrying next week's beans. The shoes on my feet. Okay, okay, let's not forget the megazons who created my astoundingly stupid 'walking path' while scooping up my data and moving on to the *next big thing*, leaving us hangin' on a highway! Yes us, US! [Shouting to an imagined satellite orbiting the Earth.] The tiny weeny me-speck and all the people who like the idea of walking, the right to walk, what do we want? Ahhhh! *That was close.*

"What, what, was I supposed to take a closer look before setting out? Oh, yeah right, sure, blow me a tune. Really, how much do I rely on this incredible device in my hands for everyday life? Yeah, yeah, deflect."

At this point, Elena was arguing with an imaginary CEO of a global tech company.

"Well, you think you *know*, master and commander, you think you know this planet. Well, come down here and walk it, take a good hard look… As for the best and brightest, what is this? Is *this* the best you can do?"

Paradoxically, it was in the midst of cursing, pain and rising anxiety, that she began to fully step where her feet were walking. She didn't care at the time for the turn after turn of drab scenery, the smell of fuel, or the stone-faced innkeeper at day's end. It was in the pain, the yelling, the fear, and the finding of solutions – a crack in the fence, a hedge to pee behind, a room by nightfall – that she began to fully connect to the experience.

The next morning, she was woken by a dream of a truck, the size of a tanker. As it roared past her on the roadside, she was spun into the air. She landed with a thud, in a daze, in a dark, dank single room, in a converted former pub, called The Grisly Gizzard Inn. It was hard to imagine its glory days. The mattress was thin and the walls thinner. After discerning the domestic drama behind her bedhead was not about to turn violent, she lost interest, willed herself up and into a hot shower. There was no soap. Dripping water onto the floor, she grabbed the tiny bar from the sink. As she washed her skin with solid detergent, she wondered if it was better to stink. She pulled off the shower head and directed the weak stream of water onto anywhere that hurt. Tired already, she sensed the day ahead would be a plod and a blur, as she stayed on the road to Canterbury.

Remaining well-hydrated throughout the day was essential, as her energy levels correlated with fluid intake, but finding places to pee became an unwelcome preoccupation. She was also learning it was unwise to delay a meal. It was the first time in her life — or at least as far as she could remember — that she fully understood the word ravenous.

After a long day alongside traffic, she ignored the delights of Canterbury and headed straight to her room for the night. The owner had left the key in a lockbox and the entrance door was up a flight of steep stairs. In an almost trance-like state, she demolished a pizza while soaking her feet in a cleaning bucket. She collapsed in a hard bed and was up and out the next morning long before first light.

It was the start of day three. Her legs pulled her along the main route out of Canterbury ignoring an ache in her calves and lower back. She looked for cathedral spires, but it was still dark, save for street lighting. She felt anxious. She pushed the persistent thought away that her journey so far had proven disappointing. Was this all a serious, mortifying mistake? Perhaps there's a sound reason why there seemed to be no one else with the same idea, and why money was not spent on accommodating people who use their legs to travel. The corridor of outer London she had navigated had shocked her and the countryside — the 'green and pleasure' she thought had existed beyond the M25 — had so far failed to materialize.

She looked for a sign of life along an unlit row of shops. She dreamt of a bacon and egg sandwich and a coffee, *any* coffee — a long-expired sachet of instant would do. The lights were out in every home. Should she call Della for a chat? So soon! Of course, everyone would be asleep, like the residents all around her. Dell would understand, or would she? She thought about all her friends and family, one by one, and couldn't think of anyone who would entirely understand. Where she was, sidestepping the uneven concrete and parked cars, there was no walking in a straight line, no sense of steady progress. There was no one about, with the exception of the occasional van and truck rumbling by, leaving in their wake an unnerving silence. The problem with this intuition thing, she thought, is maybe it will lead me somewhere where I am even more alone, where no one will ever understand.

But something like intuition had the upper hand. As doubts rose, her step would quicken. Somehow a deeper resolve seemed to be at work, as if her subconscious mind had been desperate for this escape for a long time.

And she was soon rewarded.

Whilst still dark, the suburbs of Canterbury finally yielded to grassy fields. She now needed her torch and to take care where she placed her feet, but the sense of a changing landscape and its earthy smells brought a release, and an inviting ease, as did the knowledge she was now well on her way to the Channel.

The air was clean. She savored its purity and leafy scent, breathing deeply. Walking down an incline at the start of a still-sleeping rural village, she was suddenly witness to an extraordinary dawn chorus of birdsong.

The sky was a dark blue with no sign of the sun that she could see. The melodious cacophony came out of nowhere. It was so loud and fantastic she was sure a door or curtain would fling open and others would join to bear witness. It seemed incredible to possibly be the only person for miles listening. Try as she might, she couldn't see a single feather or flit among the black leaves and dared not to disturb them by shining her torch. Head turned towards the sky, she walked in a circle in the middle of the empty road surrounded by a symphony.

As she left the village, the sun made the ultimate entrance, rolling in, opening the countryside and her anxious heart. Elena shuddered at the beauty. For a moment, she felt the sun's presence as the vibrating source of all living things. Walking in the lolling hills she had been waiting for since leaving central London, she unhooked. At first, she thought it was simply a physical sensation of muscles losing tension. She had no idea.

She stopped by the roadside. It was a boundless morning washed in dew. The purity and newness of the air. Deep green grass murmured in the light. Sheep grazed and watched out for their young. Tree branches stretched in every direction unhindered. The sky, roaming far and wide, was free at last. When she felt a sudden pang in her heart, she looked around to check she was alone and found only the non-judgmental nodding of farm animals. She nodded to the pain and opened her body to a deep and painful sadness. *And it just kept on coming.* It seemed whatever had been held within had been waiting, waiting for the moment she was truly still, away from the noise of her life as she lived it. She was finally alone, on a country road, with nothing to do, say or be.

Flooding her mind's eye were the memories of the men before, and her loneliness with Baxter. His touch had long lost its tenderness. Could she remember ever feeling so lonely in the company of another human being? The day she learned about her Aunt Bethany. He breezed in, later than the usual late, performing his routine, hanging his suit, playing music, pouring a drink, checking gadgets, looking for a meal, walking straight past her as she sat on the sofa. It was as if he hadn't seen her message. But he had.

"Sorry to hear about your aunt," he said, glancing at her briefly, his eyes a closed window. He was entirely elsewhere. "You're okay?"

The question slid out of his mouth as if a passing secretary had tripped slightly over the wheel of his chair.

"I'll be fine," she replied, her eyes raw. "Your favorite, with the salmon, from Gina's, top of the fridge. Bit tired... Might crash early."

"Sure, thanks."

She watched him pull out and unwrap the meal and pour himself a glass of wine. Before he reached for the tray, she knew he would be thinking about his entertainment for the evening.

She remembered how heavy her legs felt as she climbed the stairs, how empty the large bed looked and how she couldn't bear the thought of sleeping alongside him. There was no danger he would wake her with a hug, an embrace she needed so desperately. It wasn't only the absence of connection. His rising success came with an ever-increasing level of risk and his 'sleep' was barely there and often deeply disturbed. It was like sleeping alongside a patient with a high fever, or someone who had done something awful, and couldn't in truth live with it, despite the system of tidy machinations triggered by daylight.

One by one, she dragged her feet along the road. She felt another lurch. It was as if the light of her being was entering a cave. In the darkness, she crouched down, on the damp earth, seated by a grave. The death of Bethany.

Clenching her fists, she tossed over the side the rush of thoughts concocting at inordinate speed a host of reasons not to enter the pain. A deeper instinct was at work. She crashed right through and into the center of the storms of her aunt's war with cancer, the helplessness, the vast aching void on the phone, the shock following her death as she realized the extent to which her aunt's presence had supported her life, despite how little they had spoken over the years, and from the other side of the planet. The sheep ignored her sobbing. The onward shuffling of her legs helped her heart to stay open and move. One painful memory after another just kept tumbling out and a deeper version of herself refused to close the gate.

She saw a fallen branch on the ground and snapped it into a strong walking stick, tears flying. With every step, she hit the ground forcefully, scattering the sheep nearby. "I know *why* you've brought me here," she cried aloud. She felt her heart wrench as her thoughts turned to her mother.

Only two seasons had passed since her death. In her chest swelled a dense muscly mass. She heard the voice of Iolana, a patient at St Antony's, the one person who had noticed when Elena was unwell. Iolana, a schoolteacher, was seriously ill. At the time, Elena was unsure what to make of her unsolicited advice, but right now, like an arrow from the past, her words arrived with force and clarity. "Let go of the fear," she urged, arms outstretched. "Feel the pain, *accept it.* Befriend it. Is it too big, too much? Take a piece, one piece, another day another. But let go of the fear, the fear makes it worse." Elena dropped the stick, touched her chest and entered the black, accepting and opening to the pain roiling through her body. Hovering on the grass by the road, she felt, in all its reaches, the searing shame of rarely seeing her mother since leaving her home country, her fragile mother confined to a hospital and a care home for patients with mental illness, her beautiful, gifted mother who despite the sometimes traumatic and harsh manifestations of her illness, only had love to give. As she wondered if the pain would ever leave, its form shifted and in part began to dissipate. In its wash arose a fleeting sense of many women standing with her. She walked on through a green haze.

Passing an open field, she remembered Iolana's prayer and saw her mother's face. Regardless of the grip and funereal tone of her own reflections, her mother, in her imagination, appeared radiant and supremely happy. Elena looked into her eyes and gathering her energy within, poured her love into the simple prayer she said aloud.

"I'm sorry… please forgive me, thank you, *I love you...*

I'm sorry! Please forgive me. Thank you! I love you!"

Maternal love washed through her and in her mind her mother was calling.

"Live! My darling, live! There is nothing to forgive!"

Elena beamed with love for her Mum. She looked at the passing clouds, their shape and shifting form and the playful light. She marveled at the strange beauty of the prayer and the power of forgiveness. These simple words held for her a special quality she could not understand. And that was fine.

'That's enough heavy for one day, love', she said, to her trembling heart. She took off her rucksack, drank some water, and found a good spot for a hedge pee. It was still morning, and she already felt wiped. As she started to walk, it seemed too soon, to be moving, but there was nowhere to sit and rest, and she knew she could rest on the cross-channel ferry.

She thought of the things that brought her energy back. She looked about. It was quiet with no traffic. The walkable area roadside was more generous than usual. She hung her bag on the nearest post.

She stretched out her arms and let them fall by her side. Standing still, she closed her eyes. She focused on her breath. As her mind settled, she saw her world-self, the Elena-Lees-way of showing up in the world, relaxing on a deckchair and taking a nap. She laughed and let the image go, returning to the sensations of breathing, the cool enlivening in-breath and the caress of the out-breath, as warm air flowed gently across her lower lip.

'There you are, my steady angel, of the clouds to the last, there you are. Gentle current closing the open pores of my heart. Oh, sweet rest. I have arrived. I am home.'

She felt for a moment as if she was breathing in the energy of the nature all around her. She scanned her body and attempted to release tension. Plenty. Knots in her calves, tightness in her back, chest, shoulders, neck and jaw. Her shoulders dropped and she stood more erect. She opened her eyes and began to walk forward, away from the road, and not her usual stride. This was slower than a stroll, and she was not *going* anywhere. She tuned in instead to the changing weight and sensations of her feet with each step on the earth. She felt strangely at home. Step, another step... drifting, gone. She was off mind-wandering, seeing herself from above, the surrounding landscape, and up, and up, until all of France was in view, Europe, and on, the planet, rotating, the sun and other planets and stars.

Catching herself, she returned from Andromeda to sight of the farm fence and the sensations of her feet, pressing and releasing the blades of wild grass. She soon felt within, her energy settling, her body grounding, and an inner stream of peacefulness. She came to a stop, slipped on her bag, checked the tension of her shoes and walked on.

The fields of grass now seemed more sharply in focus and almost luminescent. She marveled at the beauty of the scene and her changing lens. A slither of joy lightened her step. She thought of lovely moments with her mother, and they rushed in. How she would stop what she was doing and really listen. How like her sister Beth, she would find time and ways to connect Elena with the natural world.

"Oh, you'd love it here Mum!" she said aloud.

People called her mother Lyn but she was Lynley, by birth and preference, a name that delighted her daughter when she had learned its meaning — 'meadow near a brook'. Elena remembered the first time she walked the blank corridors of the hospital in Sydney her mother was forced to call home, frightened by the 'noises off' behind closed doors — many of which (laughter, dropped cups, an electric toothbrush) were the normal noises of daily life. And that first trip home to Sydney from England — and countless times leading up to it in her imagination — re-entering the same corridor, excited to see her mother but unable to suppress a nauseating fear. The day came and on those same sterile walls, jarring in their joy, were a series of vivid paintings of flowers and leaves and trees, expertly wrought. At the corridor's end, the head nurse stood at the station, a cockapoo at her feet.

"You're Elena."

"Yes, hello! So beautiful!"

"Aren't they. My favorite's in an exhibition, a white lily."

"Sr Jara?"

"Yes."

"Thank you, Sr Jara, for looking after my Mum. Can I see her?"

"She's asleep, will be for a few hours yet. It's her medication. Through here."

Elena walked through the door. When she saw her sleeping face, a charge of love surged through her and seemed to fill the room. It was as if on some level she had entered the home of her heart. Her mum was lying on her side, and the details gradually came into view. Strings of grey hair across her face. Protruding cheek bones. The neck of her nightgown fringed with a ruffle. There was less of her. Elena stood still by the bed, watching the blanket move up and down, the body curled like a child. Elena wanted to scoop her up and take her home, a home near the sea. They could walk and walk and swim together and sit on the sand and talk and talk. Elena dried her eyes before walking out to the nurse's station.

"Is she eating?"

"Not as much, but three meals a day. She's doing well. She'll be up later. But she may not be here exactly."

"Sorry?"

"Lynley works. She's an artist. She's *the* artist." Sr Jara beamed, pointing to the corridor walls.

"What?! *Mum?* Mummy!!"

Elena followed the wall staring at each picture, soaking in the fine details and the visceral presence of her mother, tears reaching her chin.

"There's something I'd like to show you," the nurse said. "Follow me."

She led Elena downstairs to the rear gardens of the hospital and across a lawn to a converted storage unit — her mother's studio — all the while sharing in a rapid download how it came to be.

"She drew on the walls, you know, at first. We persuaded her to switch to paper. Flowers, trees, the sea, all kinds of plants. Your father brought all the materials. Sketches ended up everywhere, staff throughout the hospital, other patients' rooms, the canteen, until her doctor, Dr Greaves, stopped her from giving them away. It was he, and your father, who were most responsible for securing permission and funding for the little studio, neither of which were easy, *far* from it. But it was so good for her."

Sr Jara pulled open a draw and spread out a pile of pencil drawings. The hand was unsteady, erratic in places.

"These were her early attempts," she said.

Elena picked up one, a close-up drawing of the leaf of a bird's nest fern. Holding the paper and studying the crooked lines, she could sense her mother's illness. She looked up at the walls and the evident transformation, the smooth lines, the controlled hand.

"She needs less medication now," the nurse said. "Sleeps well, calmer, happier, especially when she's working."

Overwhelmed, Elena turned around. In the Sister's tender gaze, she understood a hug might be okay.

"May I?" she said, her voice cracking, her arms slightly open.

The nurse nodded.

Her arms strong.

"Oh, joy! Saving grace!" Elena thought, falling in.

"Thank you, Sister," she said aloud, attempting to compose herself.

"Of course," she said. "It's a lot to take in."

In the studio, detailed sketches covered the walls — segments of plants, close-ups of seeds, stems, buds, leaves. On ledges by the easel, were jars of brushes and pencils and artist's tools, magazines, a bowl of dried petals, and above, mounted on the wall, a framed photo of Elena and her brother, Freddie, in early childhood.

Elena had long dreamed of her Mum following *her* dreams. Sr Jara continued talking and asked about England. But flooded with emotion, Elena could barely speak at the sight of her mother's passion manifest.

Lynley stood erect, facing a plastic mirror in her room at the hospital. She was dressed in a floral cotton blouse and loose trousers. Brushing her hair, she saw her daughter in the reflection.

"Ellie??"

"Mum!" Elena whispered.

Lynley turned, stunned as her daughter rushed forward. They held each other tightly in an otherworldly embrace. To Elena, it felt as if a purity of love was swallowing the edges between them. Wounds of absence washed clean. The mind leapt back in joyful memory. She was touching the ground of home. It was a hug Elena would long remember and relive many times.

"Why, ahh," Lynley started. "I didn't know, you were here, and all of you, all of you is here."

"Yes, Mum. All of me."

A member of the staff walked past the open door, glancing at the pair. Lynley noticed and looked out the window.

"Let's go outside, to the garden," she said. "Would you like a drink or something to eat? She opened the wardrobe and rummaged in a shelf above the clothes. "A hat? Or we can sit in the shade."

"Yes, yes, yes. Whatever you like."

As they entered the corridor, Lynley turned to her grinning daughter.

"So, you heard about my hobby?"

"Oh Mum! You're amazing. I'm so happy for you. They're so beautiful!"

"Which do you like the most?"

"That's impossible."

"Okay then," Lynley said. "There's an emergency

evacuation and you have three seconds to choose one to save. Which one?"

"Oh, you're terrible."

Elena felt overwhelmed with emotion but as her mother counted out loud, she responded to the challenge.

Lynley nodded at her daughter's choice.

"Very good. You've earned your tea."

They sat together surrounded by a hush of green and birdsong and people came from doorways, smiling, serving them sandwiches, iced water and a pot of Nerada. The cockapoo dropped by for a pat. It was the opposite of what Elena had expected and feared. Her mother seemed quite well, albeit well in her own world, and medicated, and after sleeping half the day. Elena learned the simple story of her journey to artist. She didn't have any choice. It was just what she needed to do. There was evidently a good deal of respect afforded to her from the staff — a serious blessing, Elena thought, in terms of her care. But what her mother had cared about was how the art made people feel.

Diving seagulls returned Elena to the grasslands of rural Kent. She walked on at an easy pace, contemplating the life and lens of an artist, observing the symmetry of the winding country road and slopes of ancient chalk. In a medley of bird calls near and far, she heard a laughing Tern, and the confident whistle of a Greenfinch. She took in the shapes and shade of trees around her, the lay of the fields, the shoots of Spring grass. She felt utterly grateful, for her mother's love, for the windows she had opened to the beauty of nature, for Iolana and her wise and generous heart, for where she was, walking down a country road, free to feel and to feel free. Just as she embraced this sense of freedom, she noticed deep in her chest, between the blades of her back, a sudden release of muscle tension she didn't know she had.

She imagined the generations of farmers and farmhands at work, the backstage toil behind such a calm and picturesque landscape, with its wooded borders and gradations of green and stone. At a pang of hunger, she sat on a ledge, swung her pack round, and retrieved a bar of nuts and grains. As she devoured it, she looked at the wrapper and wondered if they had changed the recipe. It was delicious! She noticed the pleasure in her body and a lightness. The earlier pain and rawness in her chest were gone.

She paused, smiling, her breath slowing, and by where she sat, in the leaves of grass, she began to see countless different shades of green in the light. Her legs, however, had other ideas and swiftly pulled her back along the road as if she had forgotten to ask permission. With her eyes ahead, she wondered where her walk would take her, and her future when it was done. She wondered how it might change who she was. She had always been a nurse and was proud of what she did, the many people she had looked after, even if she'd got into trouble every now and then, mucking about at the end of a shift, or lingering too long with patients.

Doug, the tattooed librarian who tidied the bed as he lay in it, his soft voice fraying. From the Cornish coast, Douglas

Ray Higgins was ex-special forces. The porter was due to take him down to bypass surgery. His eyes searched in pain. Hana passed by and a sharp glance in Elena's direction was never going to be enough. But by the time she heard her name on the public address system, he had managed to find the words, and relief in his heart.

Elena knew Doug was married to Nell, a warm and affable primary school teacher often by his side. She had snuck in treats inside a bowl of fruit. He said little in her company, but one glance at his eyes was your answer.

A tear ran down the side of his once broken nose. He had had an affair, years ago, with a single parent of one of Nell's students. Doug recalled how Nelly had sensed things were odd, unsaid. For a while, frustrated and hurt, she had tried to break his silences, but it had remained a secret, for now nine years.

The illicit lovers shared an 'inconsolable passion' for the poetry of John Keats, and indulged in film noir binges, dressing up in trench coats and felt hats. Elena's imagination added a pencil skirt and seamed stockings, but she remained silent. Their only rule was 'no cigarettes'. A rendezvous would end with Coltrane or Bill Evans and a square of dark chocolate from Ecuador. Dark chocolate will never taste the same again, Elena thought.

Looking up at the ceiling, he described, in a mumble, one 'incredible' day by a river in rural Devon. The only words Elena could distinguish were "rain, flood, grass" and "she wouldn't let go".

Their tryst ended when the woman moved away for work

and they both decided, and followed through, it was best to drop out of touch. Husband Doug turned his spare time and attention to about the house, repairing the list of leaks and cracks and broken things, and the space between him and Nell, to more or less good effect. Underneath however, languished the weight of his deception. "There's a darkness," he said, pointing to his chest "in me, between us". He looked directly at Elena. "Whatever I do, I can't erase it." She sensed, for a moment, in his desperate eyes, and in the energy between them, that a part of his life energy was dense and immovable. But he must have sensed it too. He suddenly and forcefully gripped the gurney rail. "I *must* survive this. I must speak to her and make it right."

Elena wondered if Nell too, had a surprise or two for him.

One of the attendants came in to prepare to take him to the surgery floor. His eyes darted around the room. The muscles in his neck protruded. The color in his cheeks all but disappeared. Sr Lees noticed it all and sat by him.

"I left it too late," he said, in a low slurring voice. "Better. She would hate me."

She sat forward.

"You know, your surgeon," she said, quietly. "She's brilliant, one of the best in the country, and your surgery is routine."

She touched his arm — the somewhat menacing forearm still gripping the rail.

"Whatever you feel right now, the storm *always* passes."

So far, this was all true. The rest was of a different

category.

"Nell loves you," she said. "You *know* that. She'll forgive you… You are both human beings. Look at your pain. What does it tell you about you and your love for Nell?

"Do you know what *she* wants right now?"

He looked out the doorway. His eyes softened.

"She wants for you to be strong again, and in perfect health. That's the call of *her* heart. Right now, the picture in your mind and body that's needed, is for you to see and feel yourself *well*, in every cell of your body. You're in radiant health, with a strong and healthy heart."

And well the surgery went. The patient never did share how things turned out in the end and Elena was used to that and didn't expect to learn. Their time together in a moment of crisis was what mattered, and the moment was gone. Life and death rattled past on trolleys. The essential question was always, how do I show up each day? What is the best version of myself I can bring in the circumstances? These were the things she told herself, essential rationalizations for her work. At the same time, Douglas Ray and flying fedoras did enter her dreams from time to time, and her conscious mind too, whenever she ate dark chocolate.

She had met so many people dying to speak honestly, each in their own way extraordinary. She kept confidences and tried to listen well. It seemed the obvious thing to do. Patients came from all corners of the world and from all parts of the United Kingdom.

Last winter was the last winter for Gertie Lisbeth Arabella Silk, an 86-year-old German-English woman who had been enjoying later life in the capital, after almost 'dying from boredom' in the country. She lived in a garden flat right near the hospital. Gertie had been in robust health for her age, and for her life it seemed, until a major heart attack, walking to her local 24/7 before sunrise. A young father up with a baby spotted her crumpled body through the window.

Gertie, once she could speak, had Elena handwriting letters, applying make-up, learning the rules of Bridge, and organizing the abundant flow of flowers. They were all fake, due to the hospital's policy of banning the fresh variety, but Gertie knew — and therefore her family and friends — who made the finest silk flowers in London. You had to feel them in your hands to believe they weren't real. Elena learned the origins of tea and the correct method to make the perfect cup. Gertie, like Iolana, had taken an instant liking for her 'Elle' and would pester the preceding shift for her arrival time. Elena assumed it was because she liked to listen, really listen to people. She had noticed it wasn't a common trait inside or outside the hospital. And Gertie would issue advice.

"Elle," Gertie said quietly, between sips of a mastered cup. Elena leaned forward.

"What are you doing here?"

"Sorry?"

"Wipe 'nough bottoms?"

With a wry smile, Elena leaned back and said nothing, pulling free the tangled cable of the patient handset. She barely did those duties anymore, but she *was* tired, tired of her stretched out life and the constant pull and push of her work.

"Get out of your head!" Gertie spouted, before sighing off to sleep.

Elena had pondered this idea briefly overnight. Where else exactly was a homo sapien to go?

The next day, Gertie, barely conscious, was surrounded by family. She lay serene beneath an embroidered silk bed cover and exotic flowers. The following morning, her green eyes lively, she had some strength back. Elena found herself again by her side, checking vitals that needed no review. It had become a minor pattern, this return of Gertie's energy when her family had left.

"Out of your head, dear?"

Her voice was clear and melodic, though Elena knew not to count on it lasting.

"Hmmm, unsure Gertie where else I am meant to go, being a human n' all."

"Heart, dear. Your heart! Your body! Your dreams. Listen, they speak!"

"Ignore my mind?" Elena stopped what she was doing and sat by her. Thanks to years of after-hours studies, she was as qualified as you could be and still be called a nurse. Sometimes, witnessing a medical team's assessment of a patient, she had noticed what was being overlooked or missed entirely.

"No, but know, know it plays tricks. Tricks! But not the rest. The rest is true. Your heart, your body, does not lie. Has the real answers when you, when you need one." Her voice had faded but Gertie looked intently at Elena, straining, "but you must listen!"

"Thank you, thank you Gertie," Elena said, looking into her eyes. "I will." Elena adjusted the drip and the bedding before sitting back down by her side, her hand on Gertie's.

"And you? About you. You don't say too much when your family's here. Is there anything you want to say?"

Gertie looked straight ahead before closing her eyes.

"All said. They're waiting for me dear. And they sent me you."

Elena checked on her again after the shift ended, tidied her room, and took a moment to sit in the armchair by her bed and promptly fell asleep. Gertie died in the night.

Entering the town of Dover, Elena headed straight towards the port. A rising nor-westerly threw litter across the main street. Familiar shop signs reminded her of outer London. It had taken a long time to walk out of the capital's edges and she wondered just how many cities in so-called rich countries were like it. She had lived in London more than fifteen years and realized only after crossing on foot how little she had known it. As a senior nurse, by the side of cardiac surgeons, she had witnessed, inside the body, the evidence and toll of poor nutrition. In the shops of south-east London, where she had stopped for breaks and snacks, the junk was everywhere, at bargain prices, sold with bright colors and jingles and the cheerful faces of healthy people who would never go near a bacon butty. It was difficult to find anything fresh and nutritious to eat.

A woman of an uncertain age lingered in her thoughts.

She had walked towards Elena, tilting, shuffling, carrying a bag from the kind of chain bakery that profits unblinkingly from sugar addiction. Elena had studied how the brain reacts to sugar — akin to cocaine — and guessed from the step she had lost a toe or two to diabetes. Her tiny eyes squinted from pain and a curling lip revealed gaps in her teeth. Images flashed through her mind of former patients, sponging bodies too heavy to lift or turn without help, the swollen legs and purple feet that had just given up after years of hard labor. And her heartbroken friend, Iolana, far from home. Kind, genuine, and brilliant at parodying the doctors, Iolana understood what she called 'the living dead' and the unsaid. She would ask Sister Lees about her dreams. She wanted to know when she had last escaped the city, a question Elena had struggled to answer. Iolana believed we all suffered terribly from nature's absence.

"We have forgotten, *we* are the nature we are destroying".

Her day and night job was in residential care. Saving to return to her island home in the Pacific, she had been taking on extra shifts before an arterial blood clot brought her to emergency. She lived on a council estate "with two leafless trees and a patch of grass for dog-shit" after marriage to a local fell apart. As Sr Lees and three strong colleagues lifted her body for surgery, she died in their arms.

Elena had witnessed death, many times. Iolana's gripped her soul. She couldn't speak. Ten minutes later, in a closet covered in a blanket, Elena sobbed until she couldn't anymore.

Io-Io-Iolana. You opened your heart to me. Your

gargantuan heart. Blessing and burden. Something so deeply moving about your sheer presence. Ethereal, rooted in the earth, feet in the sea, your wise eyes smiling now from the shores of the Pacific. In this sorry world, you were not seen. But you showed up anyway, all of you, every day, in joy, pain and sorrow. Inspiring others like me all your days. All my days. The crumpled nurse rose to her feet, cleaned herself up and went back to work.

It was a breeze of mussels and salt. Instantly, her fatigue fell away. She started to hum and was drowned out by a scrum of seagulls. At first sight of The Channel, she gasped and giggled. At the ferry port, the need to navigate a huge carpark and join a slow-moving queue did little to calm her rising excitement. She stood at last on the deck of the *Pride of Burgundy*.

The simple awareness of the moment the ferry left the shore was a cause of overwhelming joy. Crossing the historic sea lane was a blast of new air. Elena felt years younger, even giddy. Inside, in the ferry lounge, she wondered if she had more in common with the children climbing over seats than the more mature passengers, many of whom were motionless, transfixed by a screen, absorbed by the virtual world.

In front of a bathroom mirror, she pulled out a comb and de-tangled her mass of matted hair, tying it back off her face into a ponytail. She added cream to her hands, balm to her lips and pondered her reflection. Another passenger came through the door. She picked up her bag to sort her belongings, trying to interpret her uplifted state.

Clear! A joy's with me I've not known, for how long... I don't know. It's you, my joyful heart, that lets me know this is so right. But it's unsettling, to feel somehow estranged from other... adults? To have left my job! I'm tired of it, sure, but it's usually satisfying, most days. I have helped to save life, ease pain. And pulling away, from my mates, wandering off into the unknown, solo, what, *to find myself?* Where I don't speak the language, and with no plan, no goal. How lonely will I be? Am I slightly mad? Is that it. Maybe I have a little of Mum's illness, maybe it's my turn.

Okay, okay… Yes, I feel it and you are true. Worst case, Hana still has a job for me, and Franny and Joe will pretend as if I never left, after the stories. Is that *really* the worst case? Oh, stop it! Give it a break. I miss my guitar. Why aren't I hungry? I should be by now.

She checked her things and noted for the umpteenth time that her passport was secure and fastened the ties on her rucksack. She left for the outside deck and found a bench out of the wind. No one was about. She tightened her coat, donned gloves and crossed her arms, looking out across the choppy water and breaks in the cloud.

Why do I think there is something else for me in this life? I make a good nurse. My work is valued. I genuinely help people and they are people who really need help.

The wildness of the sea caught her attention. She could somehow feel it in her body, a loosening, as the whipping waves splashed and washed through her. She felt a shiver on the tips of her ear lobes, on the back of her neck and down her spine. The inside of her fingers tingled. This interruption of her mind's ruminations was brief. The sensual arousal soon led to her imagining, then and there, making love on the bench. All over rather swiftly. Some lovely man. And the bench in her fantasy was much more comfortable, the deck somehow private. *Who was that?* The feeling of sex with a lover, not a stranger. Laughing as they came to their senses. But she couldn't place who he was. Either he was looking away or his face was blurred. She took a deep breath and sighed.

Ah men. After all the endings, what have I to learn?

I think I am lovable, capable of loving a good man, with time, for us. But, why so? Yes. Why does that idea feel smaller than it's ever been? Why do I feel as if my heart's expanding? This sensation of the wide. A greater love. What is this feeling, spreading all over me, lifting my mind and flying, flying across the seas, riding a great golden bird, body and wings aglow. Where is it taking me?

"Are you okay?" an approaching man asked her, with the hint of an Italian accent.

"Oh yes, thank you."

The ferry was tilting from side to side.

"I don't think we're allowed on deck, but if you're okay, and didn't hear the message, neither did I."

Elena took in her surroundings and glanced back at the man now seated next to her. He placed on the seat a leather travel bag with double stitching and buckles. Silver-streaked black hair matched his smoky grey coat and polished shoes.

What message.

They sat quietly as the wind whistled through the ship's machinery. Elena felt calmer in her body but mentally more anxious. Who dresses up anymore for The Channel crossing? Since the middle of the last century? And these days, passengers with means did not usually take the ferry.

As he unzipped the bag, his coat fell open and revealed the collar of a priest. Elena gulped. He pulled out a pale blue pencil case from which he retrieved a large hand rolled cigarette.

"Do you mind?" he asked.

"Sure. Feel free."

He lit the end with an engraved silver lighter and took a short sharp inhale and a deep inward breath. Elena's eyes widened and she faced the sea, wondering what was next. The smell she knew well from her youth and, more recently, from some of the nursing fraternity, including a colleague on the 4th floor. He slid his fingers along the joint and presented it to her with a slight twist of his soft-skinned hand.

She took in the sight. An immaculately groomed priest, not far from handsome, on a slanting ferry, was offering her marijuana, and his presence inexplicably made her feel both peaceful and nervous. She accepted, and took a small toke, pausing, regarding the spliff in her hand, and the sea behind it, and then took another longer toke before passing it back. Like riding a bike, she thought.

"Grazie mille," she said finally, in smoked tongue.

"Parla italiano?"

"That's it, I'm afraid. And I don't wish to thank you a

thousand times. I don't smoke. But I do wish to thank you, for your kindness, and to say, this is an extraordinary day... and I will stop talking now."

"No, no, please go on," he said smiling. "It's good to listen. Please."

"If you can answer me one question."

"Anything."

"Are you a priest?"

"No."

Elena slid slightly down the bench away from him.

"I have a job to do," he said, "to help someone, and I need to dress like this. I'm a financial advisor in London."

"You usually take the ferry?"

"*One* question?"

"Sure," said Elena. "I don't smoke. I work as a clinical nurse specialist in heart disease. We don't smoke, well, usually. Oh look!"

He did not turn fast enough. A children's small toy car flew across the deck and over the edge.

Elena got up and steadied herself against the rail looking down the deck. She sat back down and faced her gentleman friend.

"I would love to know why your costume is required. But that's not a question," she said, waiting for an answer, with less and less concern. They sat quietly smoking the rest of the joint until finally, padre spoke, undisturbed apparently by the tilting horizon. "It's beautiful here."

"Yes... the water's story, the sea," Elena said looking straight ahead, strands of hair whipping her face. "So many souls crossing her, unknowing, all packed in parcels, en route, with a place to go."

"And you?"

"I don't know exactly, why I'm here. I have no mission. Not one I can comprehend. I don't understand why I choose to trust certain people I hardly know but sometimes in life, I have met people who I implicitly trust. I'm afraid Father Grass you are not entirely one of those. But there have been moments, they have entered my life and told me precisely what I needed to know before disappearing. And there have been times, where I have been moved by an invisible force, or it is how it feels, and it has moved me to a place or some situation which has literally rescued me, or others, or has led to some greater good. There are experiences I have had which are inexplicable by known science, or the science I know, or by what we can ordinarily comprehend as human beings. And this same force has pushed me to leave my job and walk out of my life and keep on walking and this is where I am, on this walk...That's some pot you picked up, Father."

They sat quietly in time that had lost its measure.

He spoke at last, facing the waves.

"I'm a little too sensitive for the banking business."

"What was that? I can't hear you." She moved closer. He looked at her with gentle eyes and continued speaking.

"I am sometimes the jasmine in the wind. I find sometimes that my greatest friends and lovers are in my imagination. So why not, dive with the seagull, glide with the albatross, across forests and seas. Why not kneel at the great waterfalls and offer one's heart?"

Their breath joined the breeze and they neither moved nor spoke again until the horn of the ferry signaled its approach to Calais. Coming into port, the constant din of the nor-westerly whipping the ship's chandlery dropped away. The man sorted a file in his bag and then zipped it closed. He turned to Elena.

"My mother has advanced dementia," he said. "She remembers who I am, but she thinks I'm a priest. My brother was a priest once, in Italy; he's now in sports medicine, in California.

"I am moving my mother to a new nursing home, close to where I live. The move will be a challenge in her condition. She's in a home near Calais. Her second husband was French."

He pulled car keys out of his coat pocket.

"She loves the sea and a particular Italian car I've rented for the trip. I've created a room in the London place, similar to where she is now, with the furnishings, the pictures, in the same order. Maybe it will help."

"Surely, it will," said Elena, captivated. "Are they good people in the new home, the staff?"

"Yes, it's well managed."

"Can you visit easily?"

"My time's my own."

"Thoughtful son. May I learn his name?"

"Fabrizio, or Fabi. Fabi."

"Elena."

He pressed his hands on his thighs. He wore no rings.

They were still as the public address system blasted a call for drivers to return to their vehicles.

"Would you like a lift?" he offered, balancing warm eyes with an almost business-like tone.

Elena was silent.

"I am going to stop for lunch," he continued. "Would you like a bite to eat?"

Elena realized she was famished but was not entirely sure it was a good idea.

"Thank you, Fabi, I can't. But it was a pleasure to meet you." He pulled a card from within his coat and handed it to her.

"If you want to, just get in touch. It would be very good to see you again."

He rose and left. Elena turned her head in time to see the tail of his coat disappear through the doors. Tapping her feet on the deck, she followed the dance of a pair of seagulls, grinning. She pulled out snacks from her bag and drank some water. She savored her dried fruit as if it were fine dining, waiting until the last call for departing passengers.

6

Was there a band playing? Elena strided off the ferry at Calais. Passengers struggled with bags and children, checking signs. Elena was bouncing, or at least, her rucksack was jumping up and down. She had arrived in France, setting foot on the continent of Europe. No blur of clouds through the window of a plane. No whoosh of a fast train. It was a tangible moment and she paused as she left the gangway and felt her foot touch the ground. French soil may have been beneath the concrete, but that was by the by.

Her joy was soon confronted by a jarring sight. High fences edged with coils of razor barbed wire. Somewhat deflated, she knew the reason for the seemingly hostile welcome. Brutalities of war, poverty and suppression had sent millions on the move. This barbed barrier, reminiscent of a prison, was part of an entire infrastructure of detection, selection and rejection. As she walked alongside the wall of wire towards the town, she remembered Saz dragging her drip in loops around the 4th floor.

In the staff room, for staff, where Elena was quietly having a sandwich, Saz, officially Sarah Willoughby, had collapsed in a chair out of breath. A piece of tape dangled from one ear, revealing a diamond stud earring. After a pause, she started talking, at speed, about the latest collapsing glacier, edging forward with each point until she launched herself up and paced around the cramped room gesturing with her free arm. Elena, who had followed the news with alarm, managed to simultaneously convey interest and continue eating, with little time for a break.

Saz worked in digital advertising, an occupation she appeared to both love and loathe. Her clients, once the purveyors of luxury goods, were now charities, and she would joke about their similarities, especially when it came to the sad competition online for attention and money. But she was most enlivened on the subject of the climate crisis and her energy was contagious. She had studied how oil had copied the tobacco playbook. Tobacco companies, after learning their products killed people, developed campaigns to counter or sabotage efforts to flag the dangers. Oil majors had adopted the same tactics, after scientists — their own — warned of the catastrophic consequences of their core business.

"Sew doubt in the evidence!" she exclaimed. "Assassinate the character of the experts!"

As Saz gave examples, Elena shook her head, trying to digest what she was hearing. All she could say in reply, at the time, was "How do they sleep?" Later, she asked Saz what if anything one could do, as an individual, besides reducing one's own impact. The worsening news all seemed overwhelming.

But not to Saz. Without hesitation, she said it was *governments* that had the power to make the difference in time. They set the rules of the game. But those who govern needed to feel the heat from the public.

The demands of work kicked in, but in the end, Elena did join protests in London, wrote to her Member of Parliament, and supported campaigns online. She felt relieved to be part of communal action. It was something. And she found action in-person inspiring, as if she was in the company of co-creators and in the presence of hope.

Her efforts also cut a thin slice off the guilt she had felt flying to Australia. She had offset the carbon but understood the damage. Adopting a life in London, on the other side of the planet from where she was born, was causing direct harm to the natural world she loved.

There was little of nature in front of her now as she walked through the corridor of concrete and wire. Saz warned the waves of migration to date would be nothing compared to what's ahead if governments remained slow to act decisively.

Elena imagined a world on the move, in search of habitable land, only to be met by razor wire. She looked ahead at the entrance to Calais in search of relief.

The town's windswept streets were largely empty of pedestrians. Up ahead, in a crooked line of parked commuter cars, shone a metallic blue Alfa Romeo Spider. From a tabac emerged the sweep of a grey coat.

"What do we have here?" she said, slowing her pace. He turned and smiled.

"Well, hello."

Elena scanned for her defenses, but there weren't any. His sudden presence was a little overwhelming. She walked alongside.

"Your mother has exceptional taste, Father Fabi."

"Veloce, 1989."

"Pity it runs on fossil fuel."

"I drive a Tesla."

He opened an almost empty boot and turned to face her.

"Hungry?"

Elena stopped, looking ahead at the street. The question — to keep walking, or to stop and take lunch, in agreeable company, before many miles on the road alone – was simple enough. And then there was the magnetic pull of Fabi's company. She was flattered by his charm and attention.

"It's not far. I can drop you after, wherever you wish, to continue your walk, perhaps on the edge of town, past the motorways," he said. "I won't deprive you of your mission."

She laughed and handed him the rucksack.

"Thank you. I am a little peckish."

He opened the passenger door.

"An appetite is all you need."

As he fired the ignition, she sighed quietly to herself. Only moments ago, she was fretting over carbon footprint. They didn't need to get into a car to have lunch. They were already in the center of Calais. But only the starter engine whirred, and whirred, to no effect. Fabi looked ahead through the top of his driving glasses and tried again, and again. Elena looked away, hiding her smile. Fabi cursed and prayed in Italian. The car was not having it. He leapt out and opened her door.

"Shall we?"

"Let's!" Elena replied, delighted.

She retrieved her bag, and they found easily, on foot, a brasserie and goat's cheese salad with walnuts, baguette, and a gamay from Anjou. After disappearing, Fabi revealed he had a mechanic on the way.

"I doubt there is anything wrong with your car," Elena said.

"Really?"

"Yes, it's just a guess."

"Well, I would like to agree with you. It was in perfect condition when I left Southwark."

"There's a spell on me. I am in the middle of this walk. I am not meant to get into a car. It has nothing to do with your wheels."

They shared a grin and more wine and dessert. The waiter nodded silently, removing Elena's largely untouched plate. Fabi was fluent in French or it sounded that way to her. He was funny, she thought, even when he talked about London traffic and the Bank of England. He was hilarious. Everything was starting to hum, and more than twice she imagined her lunch guest conversing in the nude, post-coitally, lolling about a great bed wrapped in a sheet. She could hear her colleagues egging her on after too much Blanc de Blanc.

"Well, I've done it now," he said, draining his glass.

"And you mean?"

"I'm not driving anywhere for a while."

"Is your mother waiting?"

"No, I called the hospice. They know I'm delayed. My dear mother is past understanding."

Elena did not hesitate.

"Would you like to join me for a while to walk it off?"

"What a grand idea!"

And they were off. And without speaking a word, they walked together through the gleaming streets of Calais. And Elena knew the deafening quality of the silence meant only one thing. As did the collar missing from Fabi's neck. It could have been a couple of blocks. It could have been six. But at some point, they turned into a hotel, entered the lift as M. & Mme Bergenhoffer, and after a strong and sweaty digestif, she did indeed see Fabrizio wrapped in a sheet.

Briefly.

Fabi left to join his mother and Elena enjoyed a delicious shower. She dressed for the road and checked her reflection, realizing, she once again felt giddy. Binning a tissue, she saw the used rubber. An old Catholic line of reasoning slipped into her thoughts. She shook her head and replaced the castigation with an image of herself, as an older woman, looking back at her younger self, smiling. She was high, and all the flags had been tightly furled.

7

The largely featureless landscape might have interested a farmer. In the afternoon, the wind had dropped and the terrain south of Calais was unendingly flat with vast open fields, few trees and long stretches before a bend. After exhausting all thought of her amici con benefici, Elena's chief company were wind turbines and the imagined stories of passing motorists.

She considered listening to music, but something stopped her.

Elena missed the green hills before Dover and questioned more than once whether she had made the right choice of route. There were no other walkers. None. As time wore on, a patter of anxious thoughts returned with an increasing persistence, like a scourge of mosquitoes.

What exactly am I doing, *walking away from my life?* Was leaving the fourth floor entirely necessary? Leaving Baxter? *Hell, yeah*. Leaving London? Leaving *Australia?*

What am I searching for? Is it a home, a place to call

home? A reason to be?

Maybe, I will never be 'in the right place'. What does that even mean? Is it the right question?

Why am I pulled to this open road? What is this pulling? *Am I nuts?* Oh, stop it. Plenty of evidence to the contrary. But where am I now?

Where the fuck am I going??

What am I doing *here.*

To distract herself, she began memorizing number plates and looking for patterns in the clouds.

She realized her expansive view of the sky was, in almost every direction, largely unimpeded, and this appreciation lightened her step. It was the very sky she had been dreaming of back when she was pounding the streets of inner London. And there was no sign of rain. The road had been dry since Waterloo.

Over her vest, she wore a lightweight coat which was proving the right amount of protection from the chill when on the move. Light green and blue with thin reflective stripes, she was hard to miss by the side of the road and that was the point. Despite its glare, she had come to like it. In London, invariably, the practical choice was black.

She scanned her body. Her legs were getting stronger. She enjoyed perfecting her posture and stride, pulling up through the center of her body and moving with a rhythm and lightness that used less energy per step. It helped that her rucksack was relatively small and easy. She had spent three weeks optimizing its contents:

- quick-dry long tops, trousers, light fleece vest
- a large cotton t-shirt with loose woolly socks
- cotton knickers and wireless bra
- roll up hat, swimmers, and hooded raincoat
- gloves and a beanie
- toiletries bag with plasters, sun cream
- loo roll, lighter, fold-up hand trowel
- phone, charger, adaptor, and earbuds
- waterproof notebook and two pens
- headlight, small halogen torch, batteries
- waterproof matches in waterproof box
- passport, currency, 2 cards, waterproof case
- sturdy reusable plastic bag
- waterproof cover
- cotton socks

The guitar was out of the question. Elena had also decided not to camp to keep the weight light, and the other major question was shoes. Her worn-in runners were water-resistant — breathing a little less than conventional models — but it beat carrying a second pair and so far, had proved a sound decision. She had yet to experience a single blister though she had learned from her preparations to make a practice of regularly thinking about her feet, stopping at the slightest sign of irritation and adjusting her sock or lace pressure. Though her runners would eventually wear thin, she had reasoned the shoes could get her far enough to earn a break. While resting up, she could wear in a new pair. After reading accounts of long-distance walking, the number one priority was to keep the bag load light.

Elena's rough plan upon entering France was to join a walking/cycle path further south, and to stop en route at roadside inns and bed and breakfasts, using the shops and places to eat along the way. It was a quiet time of year and she wanted to stay flexible. Booking ahead would add pressure to make a certain distance by a certain time. The last thing Elena wanted was a mileage target to make or a record to break.

What she hadn't allowed for, and what was becoming a cause of concern, were the particular times places would serve food — if they were open at all — so unthinkingly accustomed she was to 'everything open' in London. In France, it was neither tourist nor French holiday season. Two villages passed with great stretches of road between them, and nothing was open, not even a petrol stop. With the weather still cold, no one was out and about, windows were closed, and curtains drawn.

Elena had water but had eaten her snacks on the ferry. She had barely touched the goat's cheese salad and somewhat distracted, had not stopped in Calais, as planned, to stock supplies. Her neck was stiff and as she tired, her walking gait lost its rhythm. Mile after mile, she stepped with an increasing heaviness and her posture began to slump. She argued with herself. At one low point, the sour doubter snarled "I told you so" and questioned her sanity. But after a good vituperative stew, 'Braveheart' arrived, declaring "this is not the Sahara nor the Nullarbor Plain. This is France, this is Europe, you have barely left Calais. You are going to be perfectly fine! If you really have reason to be concerned, it won't be that hard to find a solution."

At a rough edge to the road, Elena turned on a skinny ankle and had to stop. She found a patch of softer grass close by, checked it was dry and clear of animal dung, and sat down. Using her stuffed rucksack lid as a pillow, she lay flat out on the grass until the ankle pain passed. She laughed at the great wave of pleasure that passed through her body as a simple consequence of stopping walking and laying still. She gazed at the cumulous clouds full of light and they cast their spell. She felt somehow among them, sharing her musings with the ether.

To fly without wings
rise without form
to be
without edge
in a borderless land
wash me unrolling river
fold me in the sleeping grass

old empire of the mind
how much I thought I knew
how I hoped to understand
love's illuminated land
row row steady
unending
kingdom of the heart

At the third village, Elena rested on the ledge of an empty bus stop. Using the last gasp of phone battery, she studied the route and booked a room at the first available accommodation. The rates were low season, and the inn had a restaurant. When she saw the immediate confirmation, she felt a rush of relief and gratitude. Her evening was secure. She just had one and a half hours more to walk, with only a slight complication. The sun would soon set.

It felt good to pack away the lifeless phone despite its proven utility. She straightened the tongue of her shoes, pulled on gloves and beanie, and powered on. In the fading light, she remembered a useful distraction.

She started to make up songs and sing them. The tunes were lively, at first. To a reggae beat, she imagined a conversation between flipping dolphins. But her fatigue soon pulled her into a minor key, and it was not long before she was mourning the early apparition of love with Baxter, the summer trip to a warm sea when he silenced his phone. He had taken the trouble to find out lovely things to do and where to go. He had made the time.

Water cool and clean
clean and cool…

La la lily along
Swimming n song
Salt on the skin
La lay lingering day
nothing to say

sun streamin in
La lie long lullaby
ever my
unravelling

She felt again the arch in Fabi's back and smoothness of skin and the way he dressed and left without turning to say goodbye and how she had thought his leaving so swiftly was all okay. It was fine.

The sex was fun. It was? A fun shake in the sheets. A last gasp. *Was I even there?* Sharing a joint on the ferry – my first since uni days. Did enjoy our ramblings. What did we say? But how he left. Unfeeling yes, rude really. He didn't seem to mind how it might make me feel, he probably didn't care or even think of it. Maybe he thought I didn't care either. He was accustomed to the game. I played right along. But it doesn't feel good, no, no, it doesn't. Not for me.

Songs in falsetto. Like Christmas carols in early November, and birthday cakes at work, and life online. Or when performers sing songs they have tired of long ago, over and over again.

At sunset, her energy depleted, she was singing quietly, to her mother, at first lyricless, with a calling, floating ah-eh-ah, and words came.

More of the love
More of the love you held
More of the life
you never lived

More of the world you wanted me
to explore
further from your shore
deep water
so forgiving
so long
so far
so huge
the tumbling heart

Elena kept on, tears dripping from her chin. At the end of the film of childhood rolling through her mind, she saw her mother's face, luminous, smiling and urging her to be strong and alive to wonder and joy, and keep on walking. Elena's eyes opened wide. She swigged some water, found the headlight in her bag and left it loose around her neck. Her focus fixed on the road ahead. She stepped up her pace.

Night soon fell. If there was a moon, she couldn't see it. The headlight was too weak to see all the stones, dips and holes in the ground. The hand torch was brighter, but it cast too small a light. Elena switched to walking on the road itself, at the edge. It was a smoother, more reliable surface. As the odd car neared, she stepped away, to be safe, and to escape the beam racing towards her. She would not be seen walking alone at night. After each car passed, she returned to the road and walked as quickly as she could. She no longer felt tired. She focused solely on the task at hand, checking from time to time for the constellation of lights that would signal the edge of town.

In the hotel room at last, she threw her things on the bed, ripped open the soap packet and washed her hands, ignoring her swollen eyes and matted hair. She grabbed the room key and was out the door. The restaurant was nearly empty, but the kitchen was still taking orders. This simple piece of news was miraculous. She scanned the three-page menu, in French, in seconds. From what she knew of the damage caused, she had taken to eating meat rarely, and if so, usually chicken. But there was only one thing she could see on the menu — STEAK FRITES. The meat, lined with fat and chewy to eat, tasted like prime eye fillet and she told herself, this will be my rarely. She ordered dessert.

Elena collapsed early to bed. On the hard mattress and cylinder pillow, she slept long and heavy. When she woke the next morning, for a moment, she couldn't remember where she was. Once she understood 'a bed in France', she couldn't remember the name of the town. Half-asleep, her senses were invaded by a vivid dream pulling her back in.

Weaving her way through a noisy corridor crammed with people, she looked for a way out. She squeezed through a pair of sweaty dancers. A woman with a contorting face was shouting at her about wallpaper. She spotted the edge of a door. Heavy to open, she pulled it enough to slip through, fully expecting to be followed but felt no one. She turned around and the cramped crowd faced elsewhere, unconcerned, captivated right where they were. She followed the lit passageway into a very strange open field, what looked like a meadow of vibrating light. Elena was struck by a surge of life force but there were no people nor creatures, just a sea of animated sunshine. The ground was groundless and the moment she tried to make sense of it, the scene ceased to exist. In its place opened a stony path into cloud-covered hills. She felt the whips of a chill wind. A light ahead was from what looked like a log cabin. As she neared its entrance, the wind calmed. A wide door of old oak opened to a paneled room with rugs and a lit fireplace. She curled up in front of the open fire. As she warmed, her body fell into deep relaxation, and she felt a great peace. Apart from the dance of the flames, everything was still. Moonlight streamed through the window, and all was quiet in the great breath.

The crowing of roosters shook her from her slumber, and she lay in bed, wondering about the day ahead. She scanned her body. While her ankle was fine, her legs were sore, from hip to toe. She wanted to reach the off-road path further south before resting and remembered the effects of hot water. After a soak in a steaming low bath, she zapped her body with a splash of cold. It was enough to will her loins into gear. She checked her pack — binning Fabi's business card — and headed downstairs for the all-included hotel breakfast. The canteen style operation offered boiled eggs, drip coffee, rubbery baguette, fruit, factory juice and croissants, and packets of cheese. There were no staff about and only one other guest in the large basement room lit by fluorescent strip. He did not look up.

Elena surveyed the room and, leaning back in the plastic chair, regarded her tray of food. She felt an inexplicable joy and excitement. She couldn't remember feeling this way, not in a long time. Breakfast was a feast. The coffee was good and by some miracle the eggs were still a little soft inside, and when sliced into fingers, the baguette bread had form and made decent soldiers. She cut up the apple and celebrated its crisp, sweet juiciness. She tried to understand the source of her joy, the sensation of expanding energy in her chest and her body's lightness in the chair. The verdict was a new sensation of freedom. She realized more fully than before, since her walk had started, that her day ahead was *entirely her own*. She could do anything. She pondered the possibilities and with a second coffee, studied her map, and towns en route. She planned the day ahead, considering distances and times, and found accommodation. From the buffet, she packed her pockets with provisions and zipped upstairs. As she left the hotel and joined the road, Elena was utterly unaffected by the sarcastic tone of the receptionist slapping her passport on the counter.

Passing through the town center, the street opened into a square with busy market stalls. She bought bananas and nuts and enjoyed the sheer presence of people. There were two bakers, one on either side of the square. She chose the one with the queue and lined up for a fresh baguette. Breaking it in two, she could fit it back in its paper bag and squeeze it in the main cavity of her rucksack, which was really a daypack, sitting no lower than her sternum. Elena chose it for the wide shoulder straps, and side pockets large enough for water bottles.

As she left the town and the houses fell away, she noticed a greener grass and more trees, smaller fields, as well as many more birds. She wondered if there had always been an abundance of birdlife and she was just becoming more aware. Further along, deep in thought, the road began to wind through countryside, and she stopped, realizing where she was. This was a *D road*, one of the smaller country roads of France. Had she misread the map or taken a wrong turn out of the market?

It was prettier though, idyllic she thought, a hint of lush. Nature felt closer here, and there was no traffic. She consulted the map, and calculated that this way, the route to her room tonight would be two hours longer, with no stop for lunch. She had left the town's edge about a half hour before. She could walk back and take the faster route, but she decided to carry on and didn't think more of it. She had plenty of food and water and a phone full of charge. It seemed completely unacceptable to walk backwards. She stepped up her pace and started singing.

lumina of love, fall by me
beyond song
beyond shores
moving mercy, pass through me
beneath the stains
before the cruelty
beholden to none, none becoming
all in all
you'll have your way
no edifice, no lies
no fiction, no time

wide and slow
wide and slow

The sunshine began to feel warm and she stopped to remove and pack away her vest. Her phone rang. It was Franny.

"Elena?" Franny said. "Is that you?"

"Hi! How are you?" Elena replied, pulling back from the side of the road.

"How are *you*! Where are you?"

"Somewhere... on the west coast of France, heading south".

"But where, near the beach? In the woods?"

"By the road, on one of the smaller roads. In the countryside. How are you?"

"Oh fine. How's it all going? Are you okay?"

"Yes, it's amazing actually, to be just walking down a country road."

"Off with the fairies. Where do you get your food? Where do you sleep?"

"Well, I've been staying in bed and breakfasts, and a hotel last night, the basic hard mattress variety. There's places to buy food — this is France — and I, I'm good, managing fine."

There was a lot Elena could say, but Franny had an edge to her voice, like she was a little nervous, and a long way away, as if Elena was on another planet as opposed to the country next door. And she worried about the battery.

"Where do you pee?" Franny asked. Elena laughed.

"Well, if I'm on the road, I can hide behind a tree or hedge. I dig a hole, burn the paper, bury the ashes, double check, leave no trace. Can be a little cold on the butt, but efficient."

Elena did not add her dismay at finding the paper from others strewn behind trees.

"Girl Guide badge. Bitten on the bum yet?"

"Yeah. No doubt that's ahead."

"Have you met others?"

"Well, you know, when you buy food and travel and chat with shopkeepers and fellow travelers, nothing much. Apart from the dope smoking priest."

"What?!"

"Sorry. That story will have to wait. Can't talk for long. Walking all day today and have to conserve the battery."

"Sure, you're okay right?"

"Yes, thank you Franny. It's so great to be out of the city and have the chance to think."

"Call me if you need anything or just want to chat, okay?"

"Will do. It's lovely to hear your voice."

"Great to hear you! Take care!"

"Au revoir!"

Elena turned and there was a car pulled up right beside her. She stepped back from the road and glanced around. There was no one, anywhere, apart from the driver alone in the old sedan and he called out something in French she couldn't understand.

She gave a short wave and half smile and briskly walked straight ahead saying nothing. She did not look back. Her heart was pounding, her hearing on animal alert, her ears stretched to the back of her head. He drove off and she watched the car disappear around the bend. While she suspected he was just asking if she wanted a lift, she kept watching to check his car did not return. She battened down every violent thought and plot turn of serial killer movie, but walked at such a pace, she reached the home where she was staying that night half an hour earlier.

She sat on the edge of a comfortable bed, marveling at the view. Her bedroom window overlooked sand dunes and beyond, a sliver of sea. The room was immaculately clean and smelled of tea tree oil. She was upstairs, in a two-story house, the walls lined with landscape paintings. It had taken Elena a while to find, located as it was at the end of a long, unsealed track meandering between grassy dunes and a caravan park. Her frustration evaporated at the door. Kenzie and Ben, a couple from Zurich, both spoke fluent English and during a home tour, invited her to join them for supper.

Elena recognized the wildflowers in the bedside vase from the side of the road, and a beach depicted in a painting on the bedroom wall. It looked like Tallow, in New South Wales. A wooded hinterland meets the Pacific in a long easy curve of blonde sand and surf that stretches out forever in your mind. She stretched out her cramped feet. She felt both exhausted and grateful. Here, she had landed somewhere safe and delightful, with hints of home. She thought about asking if she could stay an extra night. She wanted to sit on the beach the next day. She wanted to do nothing and give her body a rest. She caressed the bedspread, pulled herself up, washed her hands and face, and went downstairs.

The couple were cutting vegetables and refused Elena's help. They were mid-conversation which sounded like a minor argument. They suggested Elena check out the record collection in the next room. Elena was too tired for anything and spotting a canvas deckchair through the window, slipped outside. She sat back and watched seagulls squawking at each other.

Woken for supper, Elena splashed her face again with cold water. Dinner was a pasta dish with mushrooms and sage, and local cheeses, served on a wooden table lit by two thick candles. She learned Kenzie was an artist and a translator, while Ben was vague about his work. The paintings on the walls were Kenzie's but it was translating that paid the bills. After dinner, and clearing the dishes, the couple played a tile-based board game she had never seen before. Elena collapsed in an armchair.

"Would you like to join us?" Kenzie asked, swinging the tassel on her trousers high in the air.

"No, thank you. Not capable right now of learning anything."

Both players remain transfixed on the board, and Elena found the gentle click clack clack of the tiles relaxing.

"How is it, walking by the road?" Ben asked.

"Yeah, well." Elena sighed. "I wanted not to be too isolated, y'know. Just to get my head around walking all day, and able to stop along the way, easily, be near people, grocery shops, cafes. But I'm usually alone on the road, as it turns out. Many of the villages have been dead quiet. There are no cafes, and nothing like the ones I saw in Paris."

Ben chortled.

"No," Kenzie said. "There's not much work, round here, and this time of year, few tourists. Young people leave."

"Where are you going next?" Ben said, with a glance at Elena before returning to the game.

"Not entirely sure. There's a walking route further south I was thinking of, the Alps-Atlantic trail, I'm kind of winging it."

"The Auvergne area's good," he said, stroking his beard, "but I think further south, on that trail, it's mostly roads."

He looked up.

"Used to hill walking?"

"Not at all."

He sat back, tapping the table.

"Excellent hiking trails in the Alps, when you're ready. You'll need proper boots. A good map. Good weather. Water, food, comms, company."

He moved a tile and turned to face Elena. She noticed a tattoo of a feather on the inside of his forearm.

"Would start with short hikes, and with someone. It's dangerous, in the mountains alone. The weather can change very fast."

"With someone?" Elena said.

"The hostels might be a good place to find a hiker or a group you could link up with. Or there are hiking and walking groups online. Years ago, I cycled, with friends, Paris to Geneva, over the mountains, stopping for day hikes.

Wonderful. A scenic ride, almost all the way."

He returned his focus to the board with a look of concern. Kenzie was grinning. She retrieved an ornate bottle from the shelf and poured a yellow liquid into tiny glasses, handing one to Elena.

"Thank you!" Elena said. "Lots to chew on… I'm taking it all one day at a time. Climbing a mountain is on my list, well, a small one. I had hoped, eventually, to be more in nature, away from crowds, somewhere quiet. Though at this time of year, crowds are not a problem." She looked into the liquid. "My plan is not much of a plan and full of contradictions."

"Ah, Widersprüche!" Kenzie said, raising her glass and the others followed. "To life lived!"

"To life lived!"

Elena sipped the eau de vie and looked for a place to leave the glass.

"Is a good beach on your list?" Ben asked.

"The beach?" Elena said. "Guess it must be lovely out there, you've nothing between you and the sea."

"We've an Ozzie friend," he said, "lives in Bern. She's always missing the beach."

"Were you there long?"

"Three weeks," he said.

"You made it to Tallow," Elena said, looking at Kenzie, "and stayed a while."

"Two hours," she said. "I painted that from a photo."

"Beautiful rendering," Elena said.

"Thank you. It's a special place."

"Yes, the beach… Never leaves us, for sure," Elena said, quietly. "Free, open to all, sunshine. We spend vacations, every day, in the surf, playing in the sand. Hard to recover from that."

They exchanged favorite place memories, and Ben made tea. Elena watched him move slowly to heat the pot and prepare the leaves.

Kenzie pulled a small book from the shelf.

"Do you know the Tao?" she asked.

"Not sure our guest wants to know."

She handed her the book. "When you said you're looking for quiet, your solo walk, I thought of it. It's not for everyone."

"Thank you! I'll take a look."

Elena held the slim volume in both hands and placed it on her lap. She stopped herself from yawning and noticed the weight of her own eyelids.

Ben poured the brew into painted glasses. The circles on the glasses matched the squiggles on Kenzie's trousers. Elena pulled her sunken body from the chair to sit more upright, but it was hard to follow the conversation and after tea, excused herself.

Alone in her room, she revived a little. From the side of the bed, she opened the window, taking in the fresh salty air and the sound of waves. A sudden breeze brought such a vibrant energy into the room it was as if someone else was there. She looked at the book Kenzie had handed her, reading the page at which the book fell open.

The sun in all its glory
Reveals but a passing world
Only the inner light illumines eternity
Only that light can guide us back home

Have faith
Follow your own shining
Be aware of your own awareness
On the darkest nights you will not stumble
On the brightest days you will not blink
This is called The Practice of Eternal Light

She lay back on the pillow, eyes open wide. The waves of the sea washed through her. Held by a lingering frisson, she felt a shift in her state, a kind of energetic recalibration. She had no idea what was happening. Strangely, it didn't matter too much. The compulsion to analyze and understand had lost its grip. *Aware of my own awareness. Follow my own shining.* She sat up, piled up the pillows to sit erect, read a few pages more, and the text before. But it was these first verses that had delivered the jolt.

She put the book to one side, and in an automatic fashion, readied herself for bed. As she brushed her teeth, she forgot which row of teeth she had cleaned and started again. She looked at the mirror. Seeing her reflection did not trigger any thought or reflection. She was pulled to move to the window and just stand in the fresh air. Is this a trance of some kind? Am I just overtired? Was there something in that tea?! She smiled, seeing herself standing and thinking, and felt a sense of expansion in her chest that spread to her periphery. She remained still, in front of the window, feeling enlivened, until the flow of energy within began to ebb. Pulling out her sleep-shirt from the rucksack, she spotted her notebook.

Sitting up in bed, Elena recorded the excerpt from the Tao Te Ching in her notes, reading out loud as she wrote. She hadn't heard these words before but their meaning seemed familiar and felt true. She caressed the front cover, thanking in turn, Laozi, the translator, the makers of the book, and the artist with the swirly trousers. She lay in bed wondering how many other people felt the same when they read those words and for how many centuries the words had been read.

A heavy sleep did not get in the way of whatever was happening.

In her last dream of the night, the bedroom lost its walls, and moving shadows filled with humming and song. She could feel a bustling heat and hear cicadas. She opened her eyes and found herself standing in the tropics, in the centre of a city, in front of a white domed building. An overcrowded bus trundled past and all at once, she was on that bus, sandwiched between a throng of people. The crowd opened and an empty seat appeared by the window. She sat down and turned her head to feel the breeze and it was hot. In front of her, facing away, sat a woman with a child on her lap, both bouncing from the uneven road, the mother's shirt worn thin. The town gave way to lush countryside. She stepped off the bus and followed a track through grassy fields and woods. Down a gentle slope, the trees opened to a clearing of dappled green and a wide shallow river. The illuminated water moved swiftly, splashing over boulders. As she looked into the stream, she felt what it was like to *be* splashing water. Wading into the shallows, she steadied herself with each step. The cool stream reached above her knees. She looked down and what looked like dirt flowed away from her body until the water ran clear. She felt the urge to submerge herself entirely and moved to boulders where she could hold herself in place. Underwater, between breaths, she felt the full strength of the current. It was exhilarating. For a moment, it was as if she *was* the river. The water seemed to pummel and release deep tension, and to clean her body and mind. Grief arose, for her mother, for her aunt, a fist-sized black knotty mass turning in her chest. She spoke to it as she pulled her head under, 'I accept you! I accept you!' At the same time, she pleaded with the river to break down the pain and wash it away. She broke the surface for breath before sinking down again and again, back down, feeling the pain, sobbing until she didn't need to anymore. With her face at the surface, she lingered, feeling the massaging of her body, not thinking about anything other than the pattern of leaves high above her and their shape against the sky. The sky lightened. She noticed a stirring in her chest. The dark mass was shifting. She could feel it gradually coming apart, breaking down, seams filling with water, crumbling into dirt and entering the river. A shadow was still there, left in its place, but the gnarly knot was gone. She suddenly felt lighter, so much lighter.

Leaping out, she sat perched on a rock above the surface,

stunned, marveling at the sparkling surface and effusing gratitude. When she had asked the river to clean her heart, she didn't expect it to happen. An expansive ecstatic joy-filled light filled her body and flowed through her. And it was everywhere. She felt somehow connected to everyone and every living thing and the energy of the universe, and the energy felt like love. On one level it was overwhelming, and yet, she felt utterly safe and well. She felt fearless.

Elena woke to the sound of seagulls. She replayed the vivid dream and lay in bed trying to understand. Something was different. She didn't feel like speaking and had to go outside. She dressed and in the empty kitchen, sipped some water. The table was set for breakfast but there was no one about. She slipped out to the beach.

In the sky behind the dunes, long rolls of pink silk foretold the coming of the sun. The air chilled her skin and she pulled down her sleeves and zipped up her jacket. Walking down to the shoreline, she still felt connected to her dream, and it seemed her heart was expanding beyond her body, and it kept on going. When she reached the water's edge, the expansion felt complete.

Elena walked along the beach for some time before returning to the house. She gazed at seagulls, enjoying in her heart their swooping dance. The early light cast the sea in silver and the sky an iridescent oyster blue. She swung her arms high in the air thrilling at the beauty. It took her some time to feel grounded, able to have a conversation, while there lingered in her mind and body an openness, and in her heart, a surfeit of joy. Where the sand was soft, she sat and removed her shoes, massaging her feet in the cool grains.

Who am I?! Who am I to understand this, to project this, with my mind, my human mind? These sensations, apparitions, beyond... they're way beyond me and my capacity to understand. Yet they're with me, and they feel amazing! I can be grateful, yes, mighty, and feel my feet in the ground… Mummy, the way she was, I don't want to lose my connection to reality, whatever that is. Hold on. Breathe, girl.

She drew circles in the sand.

I see you, creeping fear, over the side, off with you! Fear doesn't serve me here. I remind you, relentless agitator, you can be helpful, but you are a servant, and a servant you'll remain.

She sat back, facing the ocean, both hands in the sand, stretching out her fingers.

Thank you, thank you! I honor what is happening to me. I am *fine*, perfectly fine, giddy gargantuan, but fine.

She crouched forward and watched a line of gulls fly overhead and across the rippled sand, cruising above a long lip of rolling water. She felt like a child.

To be on the beach! There's something so free about it. So free! I can be anything. There's no one path on a sand of infinite paths. The ground moves beneath my feet, yet is solid. No roof. Only sky. And on summer days, against the waves, my body can crash, slam, laugh, dance, be victory! and against something as immeasurably strong as the ocean. And I can dip and rise and leap like a dolphin. Floating in infinity.

The vibrating sensations of her elevated state stayed with her as she left the beach. Back at the house, Elena was relieved to find no one about and encouraged by a note from her hosts, helped herself to breakfast. Homemade cereal, fruit and yoghurt and it all tasted extraordinary. She washed her dishes, prepared to leave and replied to the note. At the doorway, she turned to look again at the works of art and half-burned candles along the windowsill.

The rest of that day was something else. She performed the requisite functions, stopping for provisions and walking south toward her next stop, but her relationship with the present had altered irrevocably. It was as if she had been accumulating layers since childhood that to a significant extent had suddenly dropped away. She felt a remarkable clarity and interconnectedness with life. She kicked a stone by the side of the road and was at once kicking a football with local children on a tropical beach. Travelling in her mind, she shared a meal with mothers in the Juba market and canoed down the Amazon's Rio Negro. She witnessed the play of young mountain gorillas, and watched the wings of a Ulysses butterfly expand into an entire forest, able, somehow, to sense the profound magnificence of this world in both the whole and minute detail, and as well, the chronic dysfunction and destruction created by what seemed to her as a collective forgetfulness, disconnection and illusion. She flew slowly for what seemed like hours across the Himalayas. Someone rang on her phone and she looked at the phone and put it away. She was stopped twice, at first by a driver asking directions in French, and a man on a passing tractor waving hello and hollering something that seemed friendly. There was little she could do but nod and smile. She wondered vaguely how to say in French, 'I'm sorry, I see you, I love you, but I think I'm hallucinating'.

After a plate of beans, potatoes and haricot verts, and a heavy night's sleep, she woke the next day in a dimly lit room to the sound of heavy rain right above her bed. Her mind was clear. She prepared for her day ahead.

The shower cubicle was tiny but functional. The loft room in the bed and breakfast had an angled ceiling and low cross beams. She had to take care not to whack her head. She smelled the armpits of her 'wicking' top, incredulous at the lack of odor. At breakfast, she chose a window table, overlooking a parade of tall poplar trees guarding either side of a narrow river. A waitress laid a large sheet of paper covered with advertisements in front of her and some cutlery in a paper bag. Elena pulled out her map, a pen and flipped the paper to the blank side.

Watching the ducks in the river, rain bouncing off their backs, she reflected in awe at her journey to date. It seemed she had stepped into a broader view of experience itself, within which she felt utterly connected. She wasn't sure of anything, only that there seemed to be found there a greater sense of flow, joy and peace. She wanted *this* spirit to direct her next step. Elena looked around. A pair of diners faced away, thick in incomprehensible conversation. She placed her hands open on her lap, feet on the floor, closed her eyes, took slow deep breaths, let go of tightness, and stilled her mind. She gently posed the question and instantly felt herself drawn to somewhere beautiful in nature, high in the mountains — a place she had to climb to reach.

A zip of energy ran repeatedly from the arches of her feet to her hips and back again. Was she turning into a walking machine? She pondered her route. There were no mountains where she was currently heading. She didn't want to stop walking. At the same time, her freedom to roam was not limitless and her 'intuition' was pulling her elsewhere. She could leave the prettier D roads to make faster progress to the southern trail, but that direction no longer seemed right. The noise of the rain on the roof began to make itself heard. It seemed the moment to recalibrate. Excited, then and there, she decided to head to the Alps. At the moment of her decision, she felt a strange sudden strengthening in the core of her body. She picked up her phone and began to research. A waitress arrived with a slight swing of her loaded tray. Feeling bold, Elena attempted a little French.

"Merci beaucoup, Mademoiselle. Il fait mauvais temps aujourd'hui."

"Dégoûtant! Avez-vous entendu la tempête de grêle la nuit dernière?"

"Er...Je suis désolée mais je'n parle pas francais."

"Okay. Bon appétit!"

Elena turned to her boiled eggs, coffee, and croissant with unbridled affection. She sipped her coffee and was delighted to spot a vibrant blue break in the clouds. It was a thrill to be able to listen to her deeper dream, her deeper truth, and to know, with a little care and attention, she could walk out the door and live it.

After the rain stopped, Elena took to the road at a brisk pace, and after one hour of speed walking, found her mark — a near empty station with a train due for Paris in under an hour. The mountains were her lodestar, not another city, but the destination required passing through the capital. She found the bathroom on the platform and freshened up, combing her hair.

Paris?

The captivations of the great city on the Seine. All the old stories and moving pictures swum around her mind, mostly with a romantic theme. An idea of a song came. On the platform, a group of passengers gathered. She walked to the other end and sat behind a pillar, playing with a melody and lyrics out loud. The tune was a ballad, old Irish. She pulled out her notebook, crossing out words until she was first draft content.

Sleeping with the trees today
A song fell from the sky
Now I don't lie, not to others
running into past lovers
rediscovering all the things that drove me mad
all the while
in the long quiet
the clatter of a windy night
I feel your breath
and it doesn't matter anymore

And so, there's days my love
I take an extra mile
walk the long way back through town
smell the bread we may be breaking
by the fire I stretch out with a book
on a sofa built for two

And on, night falls gently
morning light's a child
before breakfast is done
I'll hitch a ride to Orion
no fussing, no fear
maybe you'll turn down my lane
round the sun like a lover
but angels smile
close now
beneath the trees
I am coming to rely
on the golden isle
ever meant to be

Aboard the train, she found a seat by a window away from crowded carriages and sat with her bag beneath her knees. She closed her eyes and felt the train moving. As it picked up speed, she folded her arms tightly, slowly opening her eyes. She had travelled by train countless times, but now, to see the flash of countryside was a bewildering sight. Carried so swiftly above the land she had been walking, she wished to be back with her two feet on the ground. She thought about how much people missed by not walking, speeding through their world, trapped in the past or future, numb to the beauty and intelligence of now. She wondered how many of the passengers on the train were really there.

She tried to relax and adjust to the sensation of the moving train. A uniformed conductor appeared and punched her ticket. At once, she felt more settled, with a suddenness that surprised her. Perhaps it was social contact, she thought, or was it a feeling of safety that came with his uniform, his responsibilities, or the reassuring ordinariness of having a ticket punched, being again part of a society that more or less worked. Maybe, it was just the distraction and focusing on what to say in French.

By the blur of countryside, she reflected on her revelations at the beach and just the thought of her experience expanded her heart. What she had sensed felt like a deeper version of herself connected to some energetic state she couldn't comprehend. The energy felt like a greater, wider sensation of what she knew of as the feeling of love, and when she looked at others on the train, and in her life, she thought she could see it in them too, and in nature, and in all living things. It was as if we were all beings and manifestations of love and exist in various states of recognition of this essential truth.

Purple-haired Kimi flashed in her mind, a fourteen-year-old girl recovering from her third surgery to repair a heart defect. Elena had asked about the music in her earphones. Kimi had looked at her with vibrant eyes. "It's a doco," she said, curling her lip. "I'm listening to protestors in the streets of Daraa. It's not me. It's this world that has a hole in the heart."

Elena herself had long witnessed manifestations of love in everyday kindnesses, patience, compassion, the act of listening. This understanding, on some level, had never left her, but it seemed a deeper recognition had laid beneath the weight of pain she had needed to shed.

The train moved so fast she couldn't focus on any of the details of the view. She closed her eyes to meditate and struggled to focus on her breath. Some disturbance was in the way. It was not an emotion as such but the sense of disorientation itself that seemed to be hovering, waiting to be recognized. She acknowledged and embraced the feeling and as she did, she saw at once a deeper reason why she needed to leave London.

Sitting back on the train seat, eyes closed, she witnessed her London life with great clarity, caught as she had been in a dense metropolis-wide web of distraction. The perpetual noise, traffic, crowds, frustrations, grime. The massive array of sensory stimulations 24-7, and the values they projected. The absence of nature, space, silence. The importance of wealth, status, and possession, and all its consequences, for the unborn to the elderly, so strikingly apparent in the pageant of illness that passed through the hospital doors each day. Injected into this intensity was 'life' online and its desperate cacophony of loneliness. A film of foreboding played out in her mind, reeling through the toxicity in the digital world, the imperative to capture and compel, the machinations of manipulative marketing and widespread disinformation, the minds behind it, determined to shape daily life and live on larger yachts. Media and entertainment's voracious appetite for shock, awe and conflict. How it all fueled and sustained fearfulness, and informed the noise of her thoughts, day to day.

Those diligent days, when she thought she was focused on the task at hand, and what she thought she should do, and think, and be, worrying about getting it wrong, and what others would think, as she played out the roles she had learned in childhood.

Under all this, in snatches of time, she had struggled to recover and find peace and ease. She had never unwound. She wondered who could.

This time, on the beach, after the quiet in nature, quiet she had needed, to feel and learn from her pain, she had had the chance to experience a more profound felt sense of letting go, and spaciousness, and in its wake, what felt like an intimate experience of primordial love.

The sensation of a wider love seemed wiser than anything she had ever known and at the same time utterly unknowable. She thought about posing a habitual question to this deeper consciousness noticing, at the same time she thought of it, the question seemed shallow. It had lost its potency. At any rate, she thought it was the next thing to do.

What is it that my failures at finding a partner have in common? What do I need to learn to be open to meeting the *right* someone, if and when I am meant to be in a relationship? Yes, *that* question, whose old answers have been proven wrong again and again.

A nebulous notion of 'beauty' sprang into her bodymind. Daft. As she thought about it, the faces of every man she had ever dated flashed in her mind. She dropped her head and folded her arms. It was a humbling moment.

Physical beauty? What does that mean? Isn't that meaningless, subjective? But they were not, they were not all handsome, well, wait, there was something special about each one...yes. Have I been blind, drawn unthinkingly to this notion of outer beauty?

Elena breathed deeply into rising nausea. This thought conflicted with her idea of herself and yet it also felt true. She felt herself changing. She took another deep breath, opening and letting go. She was becoming accustomed to a shifting lens, breathing and accepting and adjusting her view. She shook her head as her thoughts unfolded.

All those times I criticized others, especially when I was young! and have I, subconsciously at least, shared the same bias all along? *Oh my*. In my work, I have seen it. The most beautiful people were alive inside and had managed to make their way through life without barricading or locking down their true selves, or, when facing serious illness, they had trained courage on their demons. It had nothing to do with their exterior shell.

Iolana! She was morbidly obese. And Marco! One of the most frustrating patients. Walking into the fourth floor straight off a Roman fountain, he turned all the heads, of every orientation, especially when he wandered about the ward, gown open at the back. Exceptionally well-mannered, and kind, he lied to everyone, the doctors, the nurses, the volunteers, his visitors, and of course, most of all, to himself. It was impossible to nail down a reliable medical history. It seemed he thought it was all part of being unfailingly polite.

So *please*, Elena pleaded, why this? She reflected on the times she had appreciated aesthetic beauty, in all things, beauty that others hadn't noticed or noticed less. She would linger and enthuse, trying to convince others of something exquisite, a cell culture, a leaf, birdsong, a pattern of cloud, that long gone day in the garden of the Musée Rodin. She couldn't leave. With untrained eyes, and no knowledge of sculpture, she was nevertheless drawn by the life energy revealed all at once and in the detail. It was an experience imprinted in her brain as if it was the day before. She loved how a day off in the galleries of London left her soaring and the glorious parks in Spring and the moody river. These were things that sustained her.

Maybe it is something hard-wired about me, she wondered, an aesthetic sensibility. Or biology 101, the innate impulse to mate with a healthy specimen! Perhaps I just need to be alert, when connecting with a beau, no! Boyfriend, love, partner… And *if* when. Why if when? Well, there's something, isn't there, resonating, to stop, stop attaching to it, the idea, to stop spending life force. Ah yes, the ease of that. Holding the idea of love with a partner lightly, yes.

But what does this aesthetic sensibility mean, more generally? Maybe this is a deeper truth? Something I need to think about, part of who I am. My future? If it is attenuated in me, perhaps it is part of what I can bring, what I am meant to be doing?

The scenery outside was fast and disconnected. She looked around the carriage.

If not now! Have I not the opportunity, right in front of me, to honor this part of me. See where it leads!

People were working, scanning phones, a student slept on a textbook, a mother was trying to read to her daughter. The girl was looking at Elena who felt compelled to return her gaze. Mindful of the mother, she kept it brief, and pulled out her notebook and earbuds.

Thinking of all she had read and heard, Elena wrote a list, pausing between each new name to look in the direction of the window: Rodin, Canova, Rome, Florence, walking in the Alps, fields of flowers, giant waterfalls, Tree ferns, the Papilio Ulysses.

She stopped and laughed and returned to her menu, smiling like a girl on a water slide, thinking of all the places and sights she had dreamed of visiting. Her pen moved faster and faster.

The Lauterbrunnen Valley, The Parthenon, The Pantheon, The Alhambra, Wadi Rum, Norwegian Fjords, Victoria Falls, Yosemite, Kauai, Lake Louise, Havana, Iguacu Falls, The Amazon, Uluru, the river Ganges, the Taj Mahal, Bagan, Kyoto, the Valley of Flowers, Mount Sanqing, Niue's night sky, the Northern Lights, pristine coral reefs, colorful fish… wherever frangipanis, gardenia and jasmine grow wild. Papaya. Pineapples so sweet. Ancient trees.

She put down her pen and picked it back up again.

Spectator? Artist? Creator!

She looked out at the countryside, her mind full of imaginings and song, and her breathing began to slow. Looking back at the page, she scanned the placenames and the pull she had felt before had diminished. She abandoned the list and began to draw elaborate doodles until she had filled all the white space. A swirling melody filled her mind as she drew.

Elena woke up and felt immediately for her bag. The train had stopped, amidst farmland. She leaned forward to the window and looked both ways. There was no sign of any station. Something was odd. She looked around. The passengers, strangers, were talking to each other. Elena heard English further down the carriage. With her bag and coat, she left her seat and followed the sound.

She paused at the entrance to the next carriage. The warm voice was one row of seats away. It was an American or Canadian accent. He was speaking to a family across the aisle. Elena waited till he was quiet and then stepped down the aisle into his line of sight. The first thing she noticed was the guitar case by his side.

"Hi," she said. "Excuse me sorry, I just woke up. Do you happen to know what's going on?"

"Hi. Don't know much. We've been stopped about 30 minutes? There was an announcement, we have to wait here a short while, obstruction, up ahead."

"Okay. Thank you."

At that moment, a conductor appeared and said something to Elena in French which had the tone of an instruction. He walked swiftly down the aisle followed by men in uniform and a suited man carrying a medic's bag and first aid case. Elena stepped out of the way. The Canadian gestured at the empty seats facing his table.

"I think you're meant to stay seated," he said.

Elena had conducted a vetting scan. Late-forties professional, liked his time off, healthy — apart from sun damage. He was dressed like some of the other passengers with a pressed collared shirt, fine sweater and jeans, without the ruthlessly snug fit that seemed to be the local fashion. Guitar case covered in stickers dented at the edges — baggage handlers. She couldn't see his hands but from the relaxed way he sat, and from his kind and easy manner, she guessed he was married, and the guitar belonged to his son or daughter. She thanked him and sat down opposite, placing her things alongside.

"Is that a Canadian accent?" she asked.

"Yes, and yours, I'm a little lost."

"Australian, though I've lived in London a long time."

"Ah, that makes sense."

"Do you have any idea where we are?"

"It's less than an hour, to Paris. On holiday?"

"Yes, you could say that." She looked at the guitar case. "You play?"

He shifted in his seat.

"I'm learning. At the beginning." He tapped the case. "This belongs to my son."

"He's in Paris?"

"Yes. And you must play right?"

"A little."

He raised his hands and revealed a worn wedding band.

"Then you must play!"

"Sorry?"

"Listening to music would help calm people, don't you think?"

She took a half turn and listened to passengers talking animatedly. There was a discernable note of anxiety, but it was all in rapid French.

She looked back at him squarely, dropping her chin.

"No, I'm sorry."

He was opening the case on the table between their seats.

"What's stopping you?"

"I have a very good reason. I was once in a café, in Paris, with a French friend, laughing, and it wasn't loud. I didn't know the customs and was trying hard not to put my foot in it, you know, generally, with the waiters and everyone. Two well-dressed women on the other side of the cafe were sniping, mocking, and I suddenly realized it was directed at me. It was clear they wanted me to shut up. I was laughing too loudly. Mortifying. I would never dare to interfere with the French ear ever again."

The man smiled with his pale blue eyes and pulled out the guitar, holding it in front of her. She regretted every word, realizing her rush of story to a stranger was perhaps a signal she was missing social interaction. She looked away.

"You're in France. I think it's time you gave your hosts another chance. If they complain, dinner's on me."

Elena's eyes narrowed and she looked out at the view. The paddocks were muddy and treeless. She glanced at the guitar. She felt drawn to it. She missed playing. It's odd, she told herself, that suddenly there's a guitar in my face. 'What's to lose?' she thought. She took it in her hands and was gone, quietly tuning and listening. She looked up at him and around the carriage and took a deep breath and started to play very quietly. The family across the way stopped talking and turned to listen. After a few bars of finger picking, she relaxed. Her heart swelled. She started to softly sing. The chatter in the carriage stilled. A child walked up the aisle to watch.

Flesh of leaves leaving
no stories untold
In your ever eyes
waves ebb and flow
Can you hear, can you hear me
Calling

We can't see it, who we are
Every step we take
we break apart
Table of tree
vase of flowers
we think they're ours
wondering why
oceans die
to breathe
Re-lieve
when we're gone

Calling you
Calling

Children cry in otherness
In all the reckless rumbling roar
Are we listening
Are we here
Are we marks in a cave
Whispering wind
dust and bone

Calling you
Calling

As the last chord resonated, the smiling Canadian bowed his head. She heard clapping in the carriage. Someone shouted "Bravo!" The family across the aisle thanked her and asked her to play another. She felt the tension in the carriage had eased. She placed the guitar in the case grinning.

"Think I've been forgiven."

A man appeared and leant between them. Locks of black curly hair fell on his face and in between the twine of leather about his neck. He smelled of nectarines. He congratulated Elena and asked if he could borrow the guitar. He disappeared to the other end and the passengers were treated to a recital of classical music.

As the train started moving, the music stopped, the instrument appeared and was packed away. By then, Elena had learned her challenger's name — Dan — and had been encouraged with polite insistence to join him for dinner. He had been weaving a warmth, and a special brasserie he knew in the 6th was clearly a date. Her tryst with Fabi had left her wary of the smell of charm, and one disastrous fling, pre-Baxter, with a man 'at the end of his marriage', was one too many. She had vowed never again.

She was not taken in by the way Dan would circle around to revealing yet another aspect of the evening ahead. Nor did she appreciate his earlier pressure to perform, even if it gave her the opportunity to play. The classical guitarist on the other hand, from what she could hear, was an absolute joy. She had wished Dan would stop speaking, and realized, for him, the music was just something pleasant in the background. She noticed his loneliness, but it was time to withdraw from the campaign of persuasion.

Her unease increased as the train entered the outer suburbs of the capital. She rose and said goodbye, wishing him well, declining his kind invitation. It was a relief to return to her own seat and be alone. She watched the quartiers of Paris pass her by and knew that another city, however beguiling, was not where she wanted to be. She closed her eyes. Breathing deeply, she saw herself relaxing on a bed of grass by a river. She felt a new delight and satisfaction and pinpointed why. She had had the courage to play her song to strangers and to have had the effect, however fleeting, of pleasing listeners with something she had created. While praying he did not reappear, she felt gratitude towards Dan. Without his urging, and guitar, she would not have had the chance. And did she observe, more clearly than before, the yearnings and machinations of others?

A message in French to all the passengers switched to English. The earlier delay was due to a controlled explosion of wartime ordnance near the track.

A bomb from World War II? *After all this time?* The glimpses of street life through the train window — shopkeepers chatting, a cyclist speeding, a man waiting at a bus stop — flickered back in time to the long gone, surviving through Les Années Noires, with the swastika unfurled on the Arc de Triomphe. The grief and grip of fear. Cold beds and last days, ration cards, long queues and countless deprivations. Acts of courage where to help was to risk one's own. Life in extremis, the thrill of being useful amid pervasive powerlessness, the shame, betrayals, and treachery. Children pulled from their parents to perish alone. The marks on their back. The marks in my heart. The worldwide slaughter, the millions who perished and the millions who lost their beloved. For every life cut short, on my behalf, I must choose love. Isn't this what they would expect, what we should expect of ourselves. The cry of every war memorial. In the storm, in the steady trunk of the furious tree, lies our salvation.

The train pulled into Gare Montparnasse. Elena stayed on the train as it emptied and checked her route in and out of Paris before joining the flow of passengers on the platform. She noticed the pleasure of walking on the ground again and set off towards the center. She had lost interest in the sites she had seen before and wanted to join the rhythm of the street, and stop at a traditional cafe, before heading out of town.

Commuters were flooding home, locals shopping, visitors wandering. Thrice a tourist in the city herself, Old Paris felt familiar. She found it comforting to find little had changed, while at the same time, the bustle of the city was unsettling.

She walked to the Pont Neuf and down along the magical banks of the Seine. It was her favorite place, where beneath the Notre Dame and ancient isles, she had once dreamed of the arms of love, the rite of generations near and far who had strolled the paved embankments. The imprint of human history left a masterpiece for the senses. How many dreams were born here, she wondered, lovers found or lost, moments made to cherish or mourn.

Nearby, on a leafy street, in a corner cafe with tall windows, she enjoyed soupe à l'oignon. It was lovely to linger on the olive-green banquette and watch the passers-by. The cafe began to fill with people and lively conversation she couldn't understand.

She slipped into the street and back to the Seine. At the center of a bridge of stone, she gazed at the dance of light on the river's surface. But her heart was clear. It was time to return to the road.

She bid farewell before heading underground to find her way to Gare de Lyon. In no mood to walk out the back end of another major city, she was taking the train to arrive closer to the countryside, on her way to the Alps.

She had her sights set on Dijon, and in time for dinner.

8

A reputable restaurant without the Paris price tag, it was a full house. Elena made it through the door before last orders. The last table was tucked away in the corner, with a view of the dining room. In the train, she'd attempted to order her appearance. Brushed hair pulled back softly to the crown was looser now thanks to the bolt from the station. She'd added gloss to her lips. But she was seriously underdressed. A wicking top designed to be a layer under clothing clung to her skin and she had never felt slim enough to get away with that. Other diners were well-dressed in a manner which could only be described as effortless. Every morning, somewhere between the bed and the fridge, they passed through le couloir enchanté d'élégance. A trace of perfume in the air triggered a worry about how many miles it had been since her last shower. But apart from glancing at the state of her fingernails, she did not think any more of it. She noticed instead the cushioned seat, the crisp cloth and the soft light refracted in the tulip glasses.

Tables were ordering dessert. The conversation was light, animated and relaxed but not loud. Nobody was laughing, as in what she understood by the word, even after an evening of wine. The volume had a strict upward limit everyone respected, and Elena treated as an inviolable treaty. The waiters worked together across the floor, noticing everything, in a masterful dance of skill and timing. She had witnessed something like it before in a fine restaurant in London but never to this degree. And there was something else. The level of warmth, conviviality and ease was remarkable. It seems like a family is running this place, she thought, with a passion for cuisine and a loyal staff. They all seemed to love what they were doing.

As soon as she had entered the restaurant and opened her mouth in her best French, the waiter at the door had signalled, discreetly, to an English-speaking colleague.

A cheerful young man arrived and handed her a menu. When she asked about the cuisine, he stood to her side and leaned forward, pulling back his thick wavy hair.

"So, what do you fill like eating, fruit de mer, boeuf, poisson, canard, scallops très bien."

"Oooh yes, thank you, I'll take the scallops and er, what is this... veloot?"

"Velouté is technically a sauce. So, we make it from the roux and the stock and add the purée of fresh asparagus and herbs, and you have it."

"Oh yes, that's beautiful."

"Excellent. I will find the sommelier."

He turned around and picked up another menu and spun back.

"May I help you?"

Elena chuckled, softly.

"Would you help me choose a glass of wine, to go with the velouté et les escalopes?"

"Very good, hmmm, you could choose the Pinot Grigio. But you may prefer a Sauvignon Blanc, perhaps the Sancerre... or the Menetou-Salon."

"The Menetoo would be just fine, merci."

Later, the chef himself visited her table to find out, in limited English, what she thought of the velouté (from heaven) and the (perfectly sautéed) scallops. Listening to the sound of the dining room conversations, she was mesmerized by the sensuousness and musicality of the language, and the presence of Raphael, her English-speaking waiter, who lingered as the evening drew to a close. He had spent a year working in one of England's restaurants she had never heard of, and now lived outside Dijon with dogs, chickens, and a vegetable patch. He called his pair of Border Collies Harley and Angus. On the second glass of wine, he heard Elena's broadening Australian accent.

"You're from Australia?!" he said.

"Yes."

He adjusted his stance, grinning, gesturing to demonstrate.

"I learned to ride a horse, crack a whip and worked in a Melbourne restaurant."

"That's more than most Australians. How long were you

there?"

"Could only stay six months. It was years ago. But I know the words—"

And he was off. Someone had conveyed something by osmosis, and he was needed elsewhere. But before long he was back, reciting a poem, or rather excerpts of a poem, entitled 'Moss on a Wall', by 19th century Australian poet, Henry Kendall, with all the edible furls and inflections of the French accent.

Swift gleams across its petals run
With winds that hum a pleasant tune,
Serene surprises of the sun,
And whispers from the lips of noon.

Oh, friend of mine, to one whose eyes
Are vexed because of alien things,
For ever in the wall moss lies
The peace of hills and hidden springs.

Elena, enthralled, almost burst into applause. She pretended to clap enthusiastically. He bowed and urged her to recite her own. He wasn't accepting an excuse.

"I don't know any poetry off by heart," she said. "Just songs, I make up songs but they're simple, made to be sung." He cocked an eyebrow. She instantly regretted her admission. "Please, no, it's embarrassing!"

"Perfect," he replied. "Un moment."

He returned with a tablecloth scraper.

"Vas-y!" Raphael started to scrape the cloth, very slowly, gathering non-existent crumbs, circling around the edge of her glass. Elena spoke in a low voice. She chose the lyrics of a song she had written with a poetic form. At the time, she had penned it for a lark. Now she was wishing she had paid more attention.

Flying high till day's done
Sleeping moon's a fair
Heart so wide there's only one

Washing where the waters run
Breathing mountain air
Flying high till day's done

Mourning for the songs unsung
Fear's empty lair
Heart so wide there's only one

Wary of the beating drum
merchants of despair
Flying high till day's done

See the daughter, hold the son
Feeling love's repair
Heart so wide there's only one

For us, the call of love's begun
For nature's song, we dare

Flying high till day's done
Heart so wide there's only one

And so it seemed, her reading lulled Raphael, loosening the muscles around his eyes, and his grip on the bill. Her 'poem' warranted a toast. Her third glass turned into a free tasting session from the region. A plate of cheese appeared. She was having so much fun she didn't realize how late it was. The latest time she could check into her bed and breakfast would soon pass. When she asked about ordering a taxi and gave the address, Raphael nodded and disappeared behind a curtain.

The last guests filed out and the chef appeared. He held in the air a set of keys and gestured towards the door. Outside, he pointed at a small car parked by the entrance. Standing by the passenger door, she turned, puzzled. Raphael was smiling, a tad forlornly, explaining with nods and circular gestures that it was all a good idea. On the drive to the BnB, Elena was not sure what was going on. She couldn't quite believe it. She was sitting in the front seat next to the chef who had just cooked her the most sublime meal she could remember.

He sat forward hunched over the wheel, driving her home. His small eyes flecked with light beneath a tangle of hair. She wondered if he thought she was a food critic, dining alone as she was, but swiftly dismissed the thought. Why would a critic be so underdressed and know no French, nor the French menu, nor even the wines? She wondered, was he maybe wanting something more to happen? But there was no clue to suggest it. He looked exhausted and kind. It was just a lift. She felt a little sad and ashamed she could not converse in French beyond an effusive expression of gratitude. As the chef zipped through the dark streets, she held onto her seat and her mind drifted to Raphael, his garden, and the line of his neck as it slipped beneath his collared shirt.

The host at the back street BnB recognized the chef's face immediately. Elena understood enough to realize he was actually apologizing for her lateness, before bidding good night to them both and driving off.

Elena smiled at the dark ceiling as she lay in bed and thought of her evening, and all the details of her day. The mesmerizing walk by the Seine. Her morning on the train. The man who smelled of nectarines. She was surprised and delighted at how well her song was received, and how patient locals could be with so many tourists, many of whom did not speak the language, and why the French had every reason to think their mother tongue was one of the world's most beautiful. The tongue of Raphael, and she dropped off to sleep.

The historic heart of Dijon was a wonderful place to wander for the weary. The road traffic was diverted to prioritize pedestrians and the smaller city, steeped in history, had none of the pressures of Paris. Many local businesses revolved around fine food and wine. Elena's resources ruled out further indulgences, but she was thrilled for the chance she had had to dine so finely.

She followed a woman dressed in an apricot sweater and a slip of a scarf tied close to her neck of silken black skin. She walked with a lilt and a tilt of her chin. She held the hands of two chatty young children in spotless shoes. They entered a school gate and as Elena walked by, she could hear children squealing.

Ahead, a meandering cyclist disappeared around a bend. The narrow cobblestone street opened to a town square of such unusual beauty, she had to stop and take it in.

The morning sun slipped through a row of honey-stoned mansions and settled on the square's pavestones. She pulled back against a corner wall, checking the contents of her pockets in order to appear to be doing something. Not that anyone was looking her way. It was a weekday morning, and everyone was going about it.

A constant flow of customers entered in and out of a glass-fronted patisserie. Opposite, a gaggle of school children compared and exchanged cards ignoring a man in a suit speaking on the phone gesturing in their direction. Doors on her right opened to wafts of coffee and fresh bread, and a strutting white mini-dog on a lead. A swing of bell bottom trousers followed the pooch towards a man resting on a bench waving away pigeons with a cane. By a stone pillar, a young couple struggled to speak and struggled to stand still. Elena was close enough to see the boy's face, his earnest lip, a flicker of shame. In that moment, everything else faded away. The intensity was palpable. The sweaty fruit of youth. Before Elena lost herself in memory, the sunshine, like a stage light, lit up the step of all the passers-by.

In the moving feet on the worn paving, she imagined the steps of the long gone Dijonnais. All around her, in the well-preserved walls of chiseled stone, and handwrought detail, she saw them, living, working, talking, buying bread. She concluded there must be an enduring affection here, or deep respect, between artist and artisan, and a public who cared.

She shifted sideways to reach a patch of sunlight and leaned back against the wall. The warmth seeped through her clothes and into her skin. She felt a sensation, both sublime and unnerving, of being held, of arms around her, in what felt like an embrace of unconditional love. *What am I thinking?!* There's no such thing as angels, like I used to dream, as a child. At that moment, in her mind, came the form of a man, filled with blue light. He seemed to possess immense power, beyond comprehension. His eyes, however, were gentle, more gentle, more peaceful than any eyes she had ever seen. She felt both in awe of the mirage and embarrassed for the thought and started to briskly walk her way out of town, feeling her feet on the ground, and attempting unsuccessfully to return her full attention to the surrounding scene. She paused and sat at an empty bus stop. Closing her eyes, she saw immediately that the bustle of agitation in her chest was fear, and it was the fear of mental illness. She accepted the feeling, as she had learned to do. She witnessed its origin, and as she did these things, it lost its energy. She felt grateful, her body relaxed, and she leapt to her feet to keep walking. She looked around at the neighborhood. This time, the turn of attention was effortless. The tended council gardens, shoppers in and out, mothers preoccupied, bus drivers gliding past, the rhythm of life around her, and in her step and the movements of her body — she felt utterly connected to it all.

Hôpital. To her left, marked with a red cross, was a sign for the local hospital. Elena let out a long sigh as she passed by, and with it, the tension the word evoked. She felt relieved to be walking the other way, to be *not* starting a shift after waking to her double alarm and setting out early to allow for London traffic, to be sure she was on time so her exhausted colleagues could brief her and go home. Relieved... what was it, yes, here it was really, to have a break from *listening to patients* — a freedom, climbing out of a weight, an exhaustion she hadn't realized she'd had.

The road entered farmland and while a long way ahead, she was excited to think of the mountains to come. The bitumen of the two-lane road was bordered by soft grass, and as she noticed the comforting Earth beneath her feet, the blue presence returned.

I guess, she thought, if I can walk where I like, I can think what I like! And you feel present to me *Petrus*, yes Petrus! Where did that come from! What does that mean, rock, is it rock? Well, even if it isn't, that's it, that's your name. You're not a man, no. Not a human form. Nor a memory. It's like, you're an energy, the energy of courage. You are power, but power within. Is there something about courage I need right now? You're the form of strength and yet, you are so gentle. What are you teaching me? I am willing!

She walked on, wondering why this Petrus mirage had joined her, and assumed it would become apparent. She decided Petrus was an idea she would accept even though in the back of her mind, her 'doubter' voice — shrunken and gagged — was apoplectic. She scanned her body and realized she had lost the remnant ill-effects from the wine the night before.

How well I feel! Physically and… lighter, and more joyful, hah! after opening my heart to the opposite! There's more to come, I can feel it, in my body, in my mind where the forecast is still intermittent cloud. Do I need more courage? What am I not facing? Was it about my past? Is it shame? Nothing arose, nothing moved. I guess this is a lifelong journey, she thought, there must always be more to learn.

She carried on, walking down the roadside, lost in thought, barely noticing the lilting landscape, the soft sunshine and the tiny flowers sprouting in the grass. It was Spring in Bourgogne. In a habitual way, she began to reflect on the lovers before Baxter, and there was no shortage of stories she had told herself. She had looked for the truth. She wanted to understand. She had been sure she wanted a serious, committed relationship with the right man. But now she was questioning, was she so sure anymore?

And the answer was clear.

"I don't want to be alone," she said out loud to a grazing cow. The brown and white Montbéliarde raised its gorgeous head towards her.

"No offence honey," she said.

The cow continued to look her way.

"You probably only understand French", she muttered.

Loneliness has stalked me... strangely, most powerfully *within* a relationship. If I could learn from my past and create the conditions, whatever they were, the right fellow will eventually show up and we would truly see and love each other, just as we are. Am I high on fresh air and croissants? *What am I not seeing?*

The young man, by the stone pillar in Dijon, had reminded her of Larry, curly-haired luscious Larry O'Neill.

Was he lovely! Such a fool I was. Such a false notion, so disconnected. We knew so little about ourselves. So determined I was, to prove what exactly — that I could have an affair that was purely physical, like men had done to me in the guise of genuine intimacy? The curse of vengeance on the vengeful. Was I so low? Or was I, in my youth, exploring who I was? At least I would be straight, from the start, and straight I was. Larry was keen as custard, all signed up, we agreed, one week, just sex, nothing more. An earnest young man who loved the outdoors, new to manhood, full of testosterone, how normal was this? University days, student halls, yes, my excuse, but no… I knew better. If I'd been listening to my heart, my intuition, I knew better. *And kepow!* The punch, it came good. After damn agreeing not to feel any affection, not to let it creep between us, resting my head on his chest, he fell for me, and I had to see his face when we 'broke up', as agreed, on the 7th day. I had to see his face on campus every time after that, and I still see his face 17 years later, on the other side of the planet. I am sorry Larry. You were so kind and gentle, open and innocent, and I trampled all over your beauty with my revolution. Wilde's rose, red from the blood of a nightingale, trampled in the gutter by a cartwheel.

She imagined only good things for wherever he was, that he had found the recognition of love in the mirror and in the world. She took a swig from her water bottle and kept on walking. She remembered she *had* learned from that experience; she had learned to appreciate the profound organic beauty of true intimacy, within a deeply respectful relationship, and had been more or less searching for it ever since. Larry appeared in her mind. The image was in the future, as he was older, older than he would be, walking along a peaceful beach, sunburned nose, salt in his lashes. He was looking her way with a wily smile. Maybe he had learned the same thing, maybe not.

But there had been little to learn from Raven Jim, the fast-talking Sydney journalist who dreamed of being a writer, apart from the fact that she wasn't suited to men who wore black and were suspicious of happiness. She understood why he, and many patients she had met, had wanted it that way. He had rhapsodized about a sculpture she must see. She walked around the huge amorphous block of black marble that sucked the life out of the gallery and knew their days were numbered.

She thought of her tryst with a medic in South Sudan which ended when she had to leave. She wondered whether Michael had always been so intense, or it was part of the price one paid working in a conflict zone. His company was a complete joy, while a little extreme. But he gave a damn about people. He was alive to life. And he lived in Juba.

What is it about me and men in faraway places! Avoidance? *Bart!* Dancing on the tables at Hyde Park's Serpentine Cafe, relentless in his pursuit of the perfect curry, soaking up everything London had to offer, including me, before returning to Antarctica. Such a good dancer.

No... don't go there, why don't go there? If not now, *when?* (She sighed loudly and took a deep breath of country air.) *Why* was I so thick about Charlie, why couldn't I spot that he was already accounted for? And *that* someone else was a man? Hopeless. But don't we all arrive in the world in an infinite array? I thought he just had a well-developed feminine side. And when did the word 'available' lose its meaning? I'm not at all at home in this world of convenient semantic fluidity. *Primum non nocere* I say, and those semantics have stood for more than two millennia. I was a phase, and a home for his cat, or his boyfriend's cat. Oh, not just, Ellie. Yes, that's true, we had some fun. Oh! He was bliss on the piano. We shared our love of music. What was that silly song we made up about the landlord's belly and the passage of marmalade jelly. Enormous fun we had, in the practice room at the Royal College.

Like a hammer wrapped in cashmere. In through the door swung Colin, *who?!* Didn't know he existed, not the slightest clue, or maybe I wasn't looking. It was all over, in minutes. Though really, it had been over for a while, yes. And those strange hugs earlier that day, in between de-seeding the olives. Charlie embracing me for no apparent reason other than 'oxytocin release'. In his boyfriend strode, the silent silver trolley case sliding to a stop.

He removes his gloves and shakes my hand. Introduces himself and thanks me for looking after 'Gagashi'. I thought the cat was called 'Colina'. The real Colina was human, warm and agreeable, and smelt beautiful for someone who had just come from an airport. He scooped up the adoring creature and my boyfriend and they were out the door with a waft of amber and patchouli. Halfway through supper. Spaghetti all puttanesca. It took some time the next day, with a foul hangover, to scrub the sauce off the walls.

Enough! She focused on a passing family sedan trying to clear her mind. Poking through a gap in the front passenger window was the nuzzle of a cocker spaniel. In the back flashed a young girl's face. As the car disappeared out of sight, the fellow she least liked to think about came into view. This one still hurt.

Elena could not conceive, a fact she had accepted long ago. She knew at 27, she was unable to have children. In the months-long process of adapting to the bomb, she had come to believe and accept that nature had decided she was not to raise children, and that was that. She understood and respected the different choices others made in the same position, but for herself, she did not want to experiment nor adopt. Not in her cards, she would say. The tears now falling on the French roadside were not for motherhood. They were for her loss of a relationship she had thought would last.

Elena had always been clear with Vincent of Islington, letting it drop early on that she was unable to fall pregnant.

Unperturbed, he was preoccupied with his all-consuming profession. He worked for a law firm and couldn't imagine children fitting in anywhere. But over time, things changed. All his friends, one by one, were in committed partnerships, starting families, and as for his parents, well, they adored their eldest son and could not imagine a future without his children in a starring role. After almost five years together, it was a walkaway issue. Still connected, through mutual friends, she had learned that within weeks, he had moved in with another, a schoolteacher. Someone else was raising his children now.

A bird squawked above. She watched its long wings glide and flap as it landed on the branch of an oak tree. An old farm vehicle trundled past, its engine stuttering. The driver, of a similar vintage, nodded as he passed by. She reciprocated, her posture relaxing. Life rolls on, she thought, as she watched the tractor putter up the road and turn the bend. At least, I never had to worry about the tick tick tock of the biological clock. At 37, it might have been deafening.

"Tick tick tock, tick tick tock!" she said out loud, in a sing song voice. She thought of her age and the streaks of grey and she pictured the men she'd known and how they might look today. *I may be getting older but so are they*, and she was familiar with all the frailties of older men.

A gentle incline flattened at the curve in the road. As the next stretch of farmland came into view, Elena stopped to take it in. It was a jolt to the senses. Beneath an open blue sky, the fields had turned bright yellow. Flowers stretched out in front of her in almost every direction. She was alone apart from the tractor driver who had left the road and was bumping along a track through the rapeseed leaving a swirl of dust. She stood a minute, in awe at the sight, absorbing the beauty. As she walked on, she noticed the felt imprint of the view in her body.

Burgundy, Bourgogne. There were stories of how lovely it might be to drive around with friends and taste wine and dine and laugh in the back of an open car and lose your shoes and all that. Something she had never done and couldn't really imagine ever doing, unless of course she met a poetry-reciting bilingual waiter with a pair of Border Collies. But it didn't really add up. Her London friends Franny and Joe would love that idea. Franny and Joe, there was something slightly concerning about how they lost each other in each other, but whatever makes them happy, she thought. Who am I to chisel at the fountain?

Wow, it's so beautiful here, she thought, swinging her arms. The light in the flowers! And there's no one else here! Well, almost… There you are Mummy, smiling. Whenever I am somewhere exquisite. The presence of you seems to gently breathe in, by my side. Is my love for you, in my unconscious mind, inviting you, sharing this with you? It feels so warm. Whatever is happening, I feel you, and that's enough. It's as if an artist was up all night, just for us! You always loved France, or your idea of it. *I love you so much!*

Oh yes, yes, I know, you were protecting me. I know you knew. You found out, what he'd said, the doctor, my visits to see you, what they were doing to my mind. My sensitivity made me vulnerable, to depression, anxiety, and seeing you that way, well, the stress was extreme. I thought I was coping. Clearly, I wasn't.

She fingered a scar on her wrist.

One does not use a wrist to open a glass window. I was numb.

She turned the ring around her forefinger back and forth.

I understand *why* you urged me to travel and nurse abroad. Beth told me everything, how she had revealed to you my doctor's warnings, after promising not to, which of course, I understood. I remember how brilliantly Dr Lowski got me, a few minutes in. Concerned he was, any major stress. But nursing toughened me up Mum, England too. In the early days, those who loathed earnestness, enthusiasm, mocked it out of me. Or did they? *(Laughing)* The wittiest had us in stitches in the ward. Helped keep us sane. But banter could swiftly turn nasty or brutally bleak, especially when driven by self-loathing. And you go along with the joke, no matter how humiliating, or you're accused of committing the grave sin of taking yourself too seriously. Have heard plain bullying dressed up as witty banter, and parents, loving parents, belittling, ridiculing their own, as they chat to a friend or even a stranger, *in front of the child.* In public. Laugh it off, and I can't help but imagine what is said in private. Toughens them up. Layer upon layer. Ready for a world still by and large made by men.

Oh Mum, *yes!* Funny, my mind sees the strangest things... a world by and large made by women. I see it! Unfolding in my mind. Women seek power, of course, play the same games. But why does it seem to me, that a world, where a great many more women are in positions of influence and power, would mean more problem solving, collaborating, less ego, more listening, more *inclusivity* — men for starters, would not be patronised, relegated to secondary roles, or be victims of tokenism. I mean, what on Earth for?

I'd like to have to re-train, less people falling ill. Sharing what works. From everywhere. All cultures. Living in the London multiverse opens the prospect of a different kind of ambition. What of the pleasure of playing one's part in the ideas, collaboration, and the results conceived and achieved together. More children following their dreams. So much deep joy in doing what you love. Rather than inventing more spectacular ways to virtually — and actually — destroy each other and our shared home.

How is it I *feel* them mum, mothers everywhere, tired, so tired. Tired of the fighting, the corruption, the poisoned air, toxic rivers. Food and water they can't trust. Tired of trying to raise families single-handedly in cultures that don't value what they do, contorting their beloved into becoming performers, premature adults who can function in a dysfunctional world. Tired of children being drawn into western fantasies. I tell you. I have seen the literal heart of western fantasies and it's not pretty. And I have smelled the rancid crawl of autocrats. You should hear their terrifying offspring, in the ward, visiting Daddy. Some fears are damn healthy.

I wish we had had more time together, when you were well. I was so affected by the illness, not you, but all the other patients, they terrified me. Well, yes... of course, it was *you.* When you were first falling apart, I was so disturbed to see you like that, but I *had* to keep coming. The doctor thought I would snap in two. Now, in the ward, I can smell mental illness when no one else notices. I have a nose for the suicidal. They did worry a little about me, until my warning helped that chap in the shower before he bled out.

You wanted me to leave Mummy, and to make a life. And you managed to etch out a wondrous life of your own. You touched so many. But you didn't have *to go* when Bethany did, you didn't have to, Mummy you *didn't!!*

Her head dropped. For a while, she followed her tips of her shoes as they pulled her along. A car whizzed by her side. She looked up and the sun had lit the heads of the flowers. She stopped for a moment. With her hand she wiped the tears from her cheeks.

You waited for her. I know. Aunty Beth found great peace in being with you at the end, even when you couldn't speak, or were asleep, or drugged, and she would sit with you, in her wheelchair, writing letters until her back was sore. But you know all that. To be with family. To be with.

She reached for her phone.

"Freddie? Freddie?"

"Sis! Hold on… So great to hear from you! How y'doing?"

"Good. Really well. How are *you*?"

"Right now, surrounded by boxes, sorting out junk. Cold cuppa. Frank Zappa full blast."

"I love that you still listen to Frank Zappa."

"How 'bout you. What's going on?"

"Oh, well, I'm walking in a beautiful field of yellow flowers in the countryside of France."

"Wow! Fantastic! Who are you with?"

"No one. I'm on a bit of a walk, long-distance, clear the head, have a break. Leave the grind. It was a good decision. It feels great to be out here. Out of the city. Close to nature."

"How safe is it, to walk alone there?"

"It's fine. I walk during the day and stay at bnbs. I'm not in the woods or anything, there's people about."

"You must be getting super fit! Enjoying it?"

"Yes, very much. So lovely to hear your voice. Are the family all well? Dad?"

"Yep. Kai's been sick but she's back, full of energy. Dad's due Sunday, for a barbie. He's fishing! He's been working a lot, y'know, but right now, he's taken the week off, up in the Gulf, with mates, barramundi."

"That's great to hear. Give him my love."

"Will do."

"And a hug, a big hug."

"Done."

"Marta's well?"

"Yeah, she's got a couple of tough kids in her class but she's handling it. She has that bath you know, every evening, locks the door. I think it's like a spa thing, I don't know who she's hanging out with or what she's smokin, but it works. When she comes out, she's serene."

"So smart. And you? Spring cleaning, wait Autumn cleaning?"

"We're moving soon. Ten minutes away, next suburb, extra bedroom, bigger garden. Where are *you* living now?"

"Still working that out."

"You okay, is everything okay?"

"Yes, yes. So glad, we're all back in touch. It was great to stay with you in Sydney. Mum would be so happy about that."

"Yeah, she would, and she'd *love* you're in France. But Elle, walking alone? Not sure she would get that. The sis I know would be hiking with mates."

"That… that was a long while ago. It's less friendly over here, and friends are always leaving or working. London can… I'm sorting things out. Just needed this time away. And it's perfectly safe, really. I'm sorry, Freddie, but, I've got to be careful with this phone battery and can't talk for long. But I'll call again soon."

"Please do! That'd be great. It's really good to speak sis, let's do it again soon. And please, take care!"

"I will. Give my love to Marta, and a big hug to Kai."

"Sure. Watch out for those charming French men."

"Yes, well. Love you!"

"Love ya sis."

Elena stood still a while by the blanket of yellow. She ran her hands slowly through the buds, releasing a veil of golden dust.

9

The day started in driving rain. Elena had made swift progress to the foothills of the Alps. She stood at a dining room window. Early risers helped themselves to a rudimentary breakfast buffet, both the human inhabitants and the birds outside. Under the torrent, grass verges turned to mud. Flooding road gutters spilled onto the bitumen. Blocked by forest debris, a stream of water shot upwards. In the sky, a looming bruising bank of cloud looked ready for a fight. She felt weary. A rest was overdue. At the same time, confusingly, her legs zipped with energy. She had thought often of the mountains as she walked and had become fixated on her goal. She was not going to be stopped by the weather.

"In a hurry?"

Elena swung round. A man sat alone with his leg in a cast, crutches by his side, grazes on his face. The injured leg was propped up on a chair. He dangled a triangle of toast in the air with his fork.

"*I* was in a hurry," he said.

"I'm sorry. How did it happen?"

He smiled wryly.

"This will be the question for the next 3 months. I should record my answer and press play."

"Er, why not?"

"No, no. I'm being rude. I'm just annoyed. Hit a hole in the road and flew off my bike."

He slapped his cast and winced in pain. Elena admired the fiberglass cast.

"So bloody stupid," he said. "Riding too fast. Uphill. A bit like my life."

Elena leaned against the window ledge. It felt less awkward. She did not need to lean anywhere.

"You picked a pretty spot to stop and rest up," she said.

Nestled on a gentle slope, the inn was surrounded by old conifers. An overflowing leafy stream ran through the well-kept garden. It was where she had started her day.

"Yes, well," he said, regarding the view. "Need to head back. But I do know a way, to get an actual caffe latte, from the kitchen. Would you join me?"

Elena paused, and in the silence, all one could hear was pouring rain. She remembered the undrinkable brown water served with her cereal, and the fact she was packed and ready to go, bar the toothbrush. One coffee. Maybe the rain will stop. The last thing I need, she thought, heading uphill, is a headache from caffeine-withdrawal. This might be the only conversation I have today. The man watching her seemed agreeable. He was literally incapacitated. She sat down opposite him, a chair away from his protruding sock. He gestured to the waiter and spoke with him in rapid French.

"Thank you. Where have you come from?" she said.

"Cycled from Paris. I *was* meeting friends up ahead. Old friends. Reunion. A grand holiday in an alpine cabin. Bunch of drunks really. Is that an Australian accent?"

"Yes. Are they rescuing you?"

"No. They think I've already left. I'm waiting for a driver, to take me to the station."

"The bike?"

"Write-off."

"Better the bike."

"Yes. And you? Where are you heading?"

"A hike, to one of the huts."

"From here?"

"Walking to an inn further up."

"In *that*?"

"It'll stop soon.

"How was the trip, from Paris?" she said quickly. Under the table, she was pressing down on her lifting thighs as if to instruct them to be patient. She otherwise felt at ease, and it surprised her.

"Marvelous! I had to leave late and alone. Glad for that really. Up to a point. I think I appreciated more where I was, a great deal more, even the inside of a French hospital."

The coffee arrived.

"I'm Dev, by the way."

"Elena."

"Travelling solo?" he asked.

"No, no. My friend's asleep. He chose a good night to stay up late and binge television."

"Indeed."

"Coffee's great, thank you," Elena said.

"My pleasure. The waiter's a climber. He felt sorry for me."

"Do you need a hand with something, from the buffet?"

He grinned. "That's a big word for ham, hard eggs and stale bread." She smiled shyly. "No, thank you," he said. "You're very kind."

"Maybe they spend more time gardening," she said.

"Sorry?"

"When the rain stops, if you're still here. The garden. There's a lift by reception that goes down to near the exit, and a good flat path to the stream. Easy with crutches, though dripping wet now. The path winds through flower beds and beech trees. A covered bench at the end, by a stream with moss and ferns. You can no longer feel upset after a spell down there."

"Tempting," he said.

"Is Paris home?"

"No, no. I'm a country town boy," he said, lifting a carafe. "Water?"

"Yes, please. In the UK?"

"Yes."

"I've lived there a while," she said. "Maybe I know it."

"Cambridge."

"Very funny."

"You live in London?"

"My address is, to be determined."

His eyes opened wide.

"What a fabulous address!"

Elena turned a long spoon in circles in the bottom of her latte glass.

"That depends," she said.

"Yes."

It seemed a little quieter. She realised someone had turned off a noisy urn of boiling water.

"Where did your walk start?" he asked.

She looked up at him. His eyes looked more awake. It was as if he had decided to join the conversation, and up until that point, had been set to automatic pilot.

"London Waterloo. But I crossed from the west coast of France to Paris by train, restarting in Dijon."

"How many miles is all that?!"

"No idea. I'm not counting."

"Marvelous... So, there's no one upstairs, is there. Totally get it. The story."

Elena sighed, almost imperceptibly.

"Your secret's safe," he said, pretending to zip his lips.

The waiter arrived and cleared the table.

"Would you like some tea? Mirko makes a perfect pot," he said, nodding at the waiter sporting shorn hair, a curtain rod of earrings and a full beard.

"Facile," Mirko said, in a low rasp. "Breakfast, English."

Elena looked at the pair, trying not to smile.

"Admit it," the cyclist said. "You haven't had a decent cup since crossing the Channel."

She found herself laughing, remembering the many variations of lukewarm dishwater.

"Oui, merci," she said. As the men spoke in fast French, she realized that she was drinking too much before hitting the road. Hydration was welcome but having to pee constantly was not. Ah Ellie, but a good cup of tea.

Dev had slowly slid down his chair. He gripped the seat and pulled himself up. He was as fit and light as you would expect a cyclist to be, but his efforts to get comfortable on the plastic chair revealed his level of pain.

"Do you need painkillers?" she asked.

"No, thanks. I'm pumped."

She stopped herself from asking any more medical questions.

"So," he started, "forgive me for prying, but it's not every day I meet a young woman crossing Europe on foot."

"Yes, I don't meet many either, of any gender. And thanks, but I'm 37."

"No buts. I'm 35. We are the new young. Can I ask you a rather boring question about your walk?"

"Sure."

"Don't you get bored?"

She chuckled.

"You got me there," she said. "Yes, of course. Especially when the terrain is relatively featureless, like south of Calais. I was down to memorizing number plates. But it's been very strange, really."

She paused, looking straight at him. He seemed boyish now, his open eyes expressing a curious delight.

"It's almost as if every challenge, including boredom, had a function. It's hard to put into words. I have experienced a great deal that isn't really explicable, beyond what I normally feel and understand, at least for me."

She looked out the window.

"Right now, my first thought is how very fortunate I feel, to have had this great chance. My life will never be the same. There is pre-walk-me, and there is… something else, going forward."

She looked back at Dev.

"I am very grateful, and that's a deep, deep well."

The fall of the rain filled the space and seemed to slow. It was softer now, and there was more daylight. The dense cloud had lifted. Mirko served the tea, and placed a thick marker pen on the table.

Dev was still.

"There are stories we are told," he said. "And we tell ourselves. We can spend our lives spinning on their wheels."

"Yes," Elena said, turning to face him. "Or flying off them."

"Ha!"

She checked the color of the tea, hovering the pot above his cup.

"Milk?" she asked.

"No thanks."

"So, what's next, Elena mark-two?"

"No idea. The only thing I know right now, is I have a mountain to climb. The rest will somehow become apparent. I strangely trust that. I am not meant to think too much about the future."

"Know what you mean, at least, I dream of it," he said.

They sat quietly, sipping tea. The perfect thing to say was absolutely nothing at all. Elena found the silence peaceful and kind. A woman sitting two tables away with a man started chatting on the phone in French.

"Do you draw?" Dev asked.

"No, not really."

"Could you draw a feather?"

"I guess."

"Would you mind drawing a feather on my cast, and adding your name?"

She grinned and looked at the cast. What is it about men and feathers, she thought.

"I'm honored. Your first autograph."

She picked up the pen and started with a curved stem.

"Why a feather?"

"I'm reminded, by what you said, of something I read once. Now the thought of a feather brings me, instantly, into the present. I will need a constant reminder over the next few months. I'm not used to being immobile."

"The lightness of letting go," she said, in a detached voice, as she slowly finished the drawing and added her name.

"Very fine!" he said, admiring his embellished cast.

"I'll go now," she said.

He turned to the weather and frowned. The rain had stopped. Fat drips fell from above the window.

"Thank you for joining me," he said. "I *will* visit the

garden."

"A pleasure to meet you, Dev."

She got up. They both reached for their phones at the same time. Hers was in her back pocket. His on the table. He started tapping on the screen.

"Shall we exchange emails?" she asked. "Not sure when I'll get to Cambridge, but when I do, maybe we could chat again?"

He handed his phone to Elena where an entry had been started with her first name.

She smiled, adding her email.

"I'll message you with mine," he said.

"Bonne route!" she said, starting to walk away. To her delight, and the surprise of fellow diners, he banged the table with his fist, calling out.

"To a glorious hike!"

10

Elena was soon striding down the road, sidestepping puddles. Happy to have met Dev. Fun, light, generous, interested in real conversation and he, *he understood!* He seemed to know and share on some level what she was experiencing. It was wonderful to have met a fellow human being who has felt the same or similar. She imagined they were hiding everywhere. How could she find and meet more people like him. It wasn't obvious when they first spoke. She only sat down because he was injured. She shook her head. How ridiculous, she thought, that a woman travelling alone can be relieved and thankful that a kind male stranger, who strikes up a friendly conversation, is immobilized.

She wondered what books to read, whether she should connect with some kind of group of like-minded. Despite appearances, she did not see herself as a 'seeker' or a 'wandering lost soul'. She was not searching for a beloved leader or ideology with which to identify and hand over mind or money. Just the company of ordinary thoughtful people who have had similar experiences and met up occasionally to maybe meditate and chat. Would Dev know? There was something healthy, spacious and supportive in shared presence, something good.

Her trek on the other hand was the opposite of ease. By lunchtime, her second pair of socks were wet, and she could feel the moist inners of her shoes. Sprayed by passing cars, her trousers were damp and clung to her skin. The rain returned throughout the day, and as it broke, she would run to the nearest approximation of a shelter. Her sights were set on a particular inn in the next town south, but the constant stopping slowed her down, and she was still walking when evening fell.

Elena had sworn to herself not to walk again at night. She yanked out her torch, annoyed with herself. She walked as fast as she could within the limited reach of the light, aided by a rising moon. She kept repeating 'the town is not far', as she imagined all the things that could go wrong.

It was odd, this idea, that if you get in trouble, after dark, you asked for it. If anyone was to cause her harm, the blame might be deflected from the perpetrator. What was *she* doing walking alone at night on a country road? And what was it, about the dark? She glanced up at the sky and back to her path. It was not the time to pause and ponder the ethereal magnificence of a full moon. A memory returned of an endless expanse of bright stars on a camping trip in rural Australia in her teens. It was tainted by the moment she awoke in horror as the man in charge of the group slipped his grubby grasping hand into her shirt. She had tried to parse the two memories in her mind, to protect the wondrous view of the night sky. Sometimes it worked, for a moment or two.

She turned her mind to London, remembering a view from a loft window of the rooftops of hundreds of terrace houses, standing in the peace, watching the lights off and on of daily life. She thought of the night she snuck away from a crowd for the garden and discovered it was the largest private garden in London she had ever seen. Alone in the dark, she sat on a bench, in bliss, listening to a nightingale. She relished the shift of energy just before dawn, and how any nature nearby — trees, flowers, birds, squirrels, dew on the grass — would have its moment, its presence felt, as the whole artifice of the city dropped away. But now, now was not the moment for starry skies. She kept her sight on the ring of light leading her to safety.

With every passing car, she was lit by headlights. Due to thickets either side of the road, she could not hide. The town couldn't have been more than a mile away. She thought of running on the uneven surface of stones and dust. She kept a brisk walk and a faster heart. Not long now.

From behind it came, the sound of a bass guitar. It was getting louder. Fear and adrenaline surged through her body. A long car drove by, very slowly, blasting rock music. She heard a young man's shout. She faced straight ahead, and from her peripheral vision, she could make out a driver and at least two passengers in a large sedan, both looking her way, one holding a beer bottle. He held it by the neck. In the headlight beam, she scanned the surroundings. Up ahead, was a rise in the road. Once the car crawled out of view, she sprinted across the road, scanning with her torch for a break in the foliage. There was none. At what looked like the weakest point, she bumped and broke and pushed her way through, shielding her eyes with her folded arm and ignoring the whips and scratches. Her heart was thumping. She didn't register any pain. A few metres in, where the hedge thinned out, she turned to track parallel to the road. Keeping her arm bent in front of her eyes, she used the other, gripping the torch cylinder, to try to break her path, simultaneously keeping the ray of light facing downwards. While the torch was too small to be much use, it did cast enough light to avoid hitting trees or tripping over roots. She was climbing uphill and at the crest, she could hear it. She stopped, fumbling to turn off the torch, and stood still, panting, in the dark. Through the trees, on a side road up ahead, she could see a stream of headlights, stationery, facing the road on which she had been walking. But what terrified her, was the *music* coming from the car — the same bass guitar. She spun around in the opposite direction. Torch on and down, arm in front, she shoved her way faster through the brush. She could feel sharp edges slapping her body and cutting the skin on her arms and face, but she was too scared to slow. She didn't pause until the music was gone.

Jumping a fence, she entered a woodland criss-crossed by paths and it was far easier to make her way. She used the light now with abandon. She noticed the trees and branches, the leaves beneath her feet. The woods came to an abrupt halt at a clearing and a large vineyard.

She walked along a path between the vines. It was uneven with lumps of soil, dips and breaks but it was so easy compared to where she had been, and she moved at a pace. In the distance was a well-lit house with lights on, inside and out. As she neared, she turned off the torch and paused, adjusting her eyes to the moonlight. She could see enough to walk slowly through the last field towards the house. A boy crossed her path up ahead. He seemed to come out of nowhere. He was about nine, ten. He didn't see her and was carrying a box towards his home.

She looked across from where he'd been walking and could make out a large shed. She crept towards it, placing each foot on a patch of dirt, trying to avoid twigs and leaves. Behind its back wall, away from the house, she listened for any life. Apart from a few distant bird chirps, she heard nothing. She listened again at the barn door, and it was quiet. She opened the door just enough to fit herself and her backpack and stood inside the entrance. It was dark and with her fading torch, she scanned the space.

In the middle of the concrete floor was a disassembled car, behind a tool bench. To her right, a wall of shelving and rows of bottles stretched into the rafters. To her left was a raised wooden platform, almost half the length of the shed. A ladder tilted against its near side. The deck was bordered by knotted rope. Above the deck, moonlight fell through shutters on a roof window.

Every rung on the ladder creaked. At the top, she found a children's den, with a trainset, games and books, a paneled floor scattered with little cars and balls and plastic pieces, discarded cups and a sofa. Messy but not dusty. The rope barrier led to a gleaming ship's wheel. A telescope pointed to the skylight. She descended the ladder and slipped outside and around the back of the shed for a pee. She walked to the edge, in sight of the house. It was quiet. The outside light on the house was out.

Time to sleep. She didn't want to bother the family, and attempt to explain, in useless French, an incident that never happened. She knew she had been right to be fearful, and to act as she did, and the *last* thing she needed was someone to look at her with incredulity, wondering if this strange woman walking alone at night was 'okay'. She made her way back up the ladder, released her rucksack, found her phone, set a vibrating alarm, and collapsed on the sofa. She curled into a ball, stroking a wet scratch on her face. She was exhausted. A sharp pang of loneliness twisted in her chest.

She thought of her father and Freddie, how far away they were, and how far away she was from anyone she knew. *I took care, Freddie.* She investigated a lump beneath her side and pulled out a stuffed soft toy. It was a rabbit, with ears far too long for an actual rabbit and large cracked eyes. Its fur was soft and worn, resewn at the seams. She pulled down the sofa covering and wrapped it around herself and the rabbit and fell swiftly asleep.

She woke before the alarm. When she realized where she was, she sat up abruptly in the half-light and scanned the shed. Ignoring the soreness and fatigue, she was up, down the ladder, and outside. She crept passed the sleeping house, down the driveway and out to the road. Her body, stiff at first, was achy and her hands badly scratched. But crouched under an innocent tree, the feel of wet grass on her butt was a delight. It was morning, and she was safe and back on her own two feet.

Walking down the empty road, too early for traffic, her body loosened. She breathed in deeply the crisp, clean air, and its promise of a new day. Strolling amid a flurry of birdsong and a lightening sky, she thought of how fortunate she was, how beautiful the day seemed, and she pictured the still sleeping young boy who loved le petit lapin.

The town was open by the time she arrived but too small to be bustling. She sat partially hidden on the steps of a church. From her vantage point behind the cemetery yard, she could observe the passers-by and spot when the pharmacy opened.

Ignoring the looks of the perfectly groomed cashier, she purchased cotton wool, wound wash, and a bandage for her hands. In the corner of the store was a rack of reading glasses and she used the tiny mirror to inspect her face. It was dirty with a dried scratch down her cheek but nothing deep. Her hair though made her smile. She pulled the brush out of her rucksack and tried to tame it. After completing repairs, she dumped the rubbish in the bin outside and made her way to the Inn. The jingling bell on the entrance door sounded friendly and she was soon standing in a hot shower with the promise of freshly baked bread and eggs.

Elena spent the remainder of the day at rest. She took a bath, practiced chi kung and a limited set of her exercises, sorted through her kit, replaced batteries, and wrote letters to Hana and her brother, sharing news of the kind that wouldn't raise any flags. Her room was on the second floor and overlooked the main street. Now and then she would peer through the windows at the small-town life.

At lunchtime, when a group of young men passed by, she withdrew behind the shutters and sat on the bed. She felt scared at first, but in that one glimpse, she saw the clunkiness and rigidity of their bodies. She wondered how their outward manner might reflect their inner life, peer pressure, parental expectations, exams, hormones, social media, society's expectations. The way they regarded each other though, and mirrored each other's physicality, revealed a shared history. They were in it together. Her own anxious feelings however soon drew her attention into *her* body. Straight away, she could see the tension. Like a physical version of static noise on the radio, a disturbing irritation rustled in her contracted chest. She let her hands relax by her side and fully felt and accepted the anxiety. As she did, the energy expanded and gradually dissipated until her chest was clear. It felt wonderful! As was now habitual, a wash of gratitude flowed through her.

She thought of young boys learning from their fathers, who themselves learned the same, and the countless ways society gave men tacit permission, and sometimes encouragement, to harm women and girls, from the snap judgements, demeaning regard and exclusion, right through the scale to violence. She felt compassion for young boys and lost young men trying to find their footing, to find love and acceptance, and a sense of purpose. Her eyes began to fill with tears.

She was about to move when she sensed her mum, her mum's fear. What is there to learn here, Elena wondered. Things are now, the way they are now. She considered her situation and made a decision. She was going to try to be as prepared as possible in advance to avoid having to walk alone at night, but at the same time, not to let the rule or forethought impede her appreciation of the night. In her imagination, her Mum was still nervous. But Beth smiled. '*Strong* Elle, you were strong, you made good decisions and now you're safe'. At these words, the face of her mother relaxed a little. Elena thought of the truth in that, and as she did, an insight opened. She remembered the deep signal her body had sent her when she awoke in the rain the day before. *It had told her to rest.* But she had become fixated on her goal. Fixation seemed to be a creature of the mind, while the *feeling* of an intuitive spirit was a fluid energy and more loving pointer than legislator. Her lens drew wide. She felt to be a humble witness to the great play of life unfolding all the time, in every moment, which seemed, all at once, to render as futile any analysis with her human mind, or at the very least counting on one's conclusions as absolutes. She thought of the peril of the day before and how it taught her things that she wouldn't have learned if she was still relaxing by the mossy stream drinking perfect tea. She fell back on the bed laughing.

11

Walking up the foothills of the Alps was surprisingly easy. Elena barely noticed the incline. It reminded of her of being a passenger in a plane, in undetectably slow descent, but the other way round. Her legs were also strong, averaging 20 to 22 miles a day, 10 to 15 if it rained, 25 miles with a chunk of protein. Her thighs felt like engines.

The rain hung around. Walking in it had proven a major fail and had slowed her down. It had taken nearly a week to walk from Dijon. While her coat was waterproof, her trousers and socks were not and passing traffic paid no regard. She had ditched the hand bandages; they were useless wet and the cuts superficial. If there was shelter, she would stop until the rain ran out. Shed. Gas station. A tree with fat leaves. But she had had few wet days overall.

As the hills steepened, her progress slowed but she kept a steady pace. She was heading for a roadside inn at the junction of a popular mountain trek. The trail was known for its scenic views and at its end was a lodge for hikers.

Near the end of a day's walking uphill, she caught sight of the stucco walls and chimney smoke of L'Auberge René, her bed for the night. She was so thrilled to see it, she ignored the fatigue and picked up her pace. When she learned the kitchen was open, her tiredness evaporated. The type of meals on offer had been shifting. The higher the altitude, the greater the proportion of meat, cheese and potatoes.

Her room was tiny but warm, with a door to a large, white-tiled bathroom shared by the adjacent room. It had a tub, two sinks, a separate shower and loo, and a bright blue wooden chair. She locked the neighbor's door, whipped open the bath taps and started singing. She was finally leaving passing cars and would be hiking in the glorious Alps. As the bath filled fast with a powerful jet, she sat on the chair and pulled off her shoes and socks. Her left big toenail was black, the whole nail. The rain, she thought, it must have been the rain. I stopped noticing my feet.

She left her clothes on the bed and stepped into the hot water. It was full, far higher than her normal self-imposed eco level. As she lay back slowly, she could feel the heat relax her muscles. The black toe bobbed above the water. She held each foot in turn, massaging the arches, sending water over the rim. Lying back, she marveled at the state of her hands and arms. The scratches were considerable but that was not the reason. The eczema that had plagued her for the last few years was almost entirely gone. Not once could she remember a moment on the walk when her skin had been itchy. Clasping her hands at the surface, she clapped water between the palms to create an upwards squirt in time with her song. After several tries, she reached almost a meter above the bath. There was a rap at the door to the adjacent room.

"Hey!"

Elena jumped.

"Hi," she replied, half out of the bath reaching for the towel, sending more water onto the floor. She gasped at the mess.

"Not everyone's an Al Green fan."

The accent was American with the slackness and slur of inebriation.

"Oh sorry! A bit loud."

"No, it's fine. You're not loud. Like your voice. It was my ex, my ex loved Al Green."

"You need the bathroom?"

"No, no, you're good."

"Almost done."

"All good. Take your time."

Elena emptied some of the bath water. With her hands holding on to the sides she sank in and out of the hot pond, her whole body under the surface, including her head. She leaned against the bath watching the water settle to stillness. She pulled the plug and watched the level descend. She felt heavy with fatigue and excited about her climb the next day. She restored the bathroom, dressed in a towel, and unlocked the latch to the guest's door.

"All yours!"

"Thank you!"

The door swung open.

"I lied. Busting."

"Sorry!"

"All good," she said closing the toilet door with a bang. "I'm Celia," she called out.

"Hi Celia, I'm Elena."

"Good night Elena."

"Good night to you!"

Elena's bed had a patchwork quilt over a duvet, and she snuggled in and hugged a pillow thinking of the mountain beneath her. She heard a tentative knock on the door to the bathroom.

"Elena?"

The door opened a few inches.

"Sorry to bother you. Just about to light a j, if you'd like to partake."

"No, but thank you."

"Or a swig of something? I have a collection." Celia wore a loose t-shirt and long earrings. She clasped the front of her t-shirt as if she was holding on.

"I'm up early tomorrow," Elena said, "and need my wits about me. But thank you."

Celia stood still, relatively speaking, trying to balance on two feet.

"Are you okay?" Elena asked.

The door opened a little wider as Celia tilted to the side. Audibly, she took a deep breath and pulled herself upright.

"Yeah. Sorry, I won't bother." She started to close the door and paused. "Can I just ask you one question?" she said.

"Sure."

Elena, now lit by the bathroom light, stayed still, lying in bed. Celia sighed, looking towards the window.

"I came here to think," she said, pausing.

"And every time, getting high, getting up high, helps me, remember. Remember what's what, what matters. Colorado. I'm from Colorado."

"Colorado," Elena repeated, from her pillow, watching, listening, and at the same time, wondering how much of the moment Celia would remember the next day, and whether it mattered. Celia leaned against the door frame.

"But sometimes, well, this time, what's on the table, is the entire life I'm not leading."

Celia waved her arm in the air and looked at Elena. Elena said nothing. Celia seemed to be waiting for an answer.

"I hear you," Elena said.

Celia looked ahead, stepping into the room.

"Invested," she said emphatically, making a gesture resembling an upper cut, "invested in my wrong life. Knew it. Could feel it. Could feel this shit was coming. Anyways."

She looked at Elena.

"Vodka? Dope, meds, chocolate, cookies, oh yeah and downstairs... a supply of Italian hazelnut ice-cream."

Elena smiled.

"Anyways," she continued, straightening her posture, "the question. I think, I'm meant to live a life *no one* would get. I'd lose a great deal. So, what the hell am I supposed to do? I'm sorry, but sometimes it helps me to ask total strangers the biggies. It's a survey. I won't jump on your answer."

"Are you saying you need to ask the question out loud to people who are not part of your world," Elena said.

"Yes."

"You are asking the question."

"Yes?"

"Something is pulling you to ask the question, a question that takes courage to ask, and you know, in your heart, the only person who can answer it is you. But I wonder, do you remember *ever* making good decisions drinking, or stoned, or late at night, when you're tired, and everything seems too much?"

Celia smiled.

"You know the beautiful handmade quilt on your bed?" Elena continued.

"Yes, it's dreamy."

"Made with love. Maybe, you might feel a bit better if you drink some water, hop into bed and imagine the people who made that quilt. Imagine all the love in the world is inside that quilt, snuggle beneath it like a child, a safe and loved child. Save the questioning, for when you are fresh and clear, relaxing in nature, undistracted, and you're able to listen to your real bodymind."

Celia paused and looked at Elena.

"I knew I needed to knock on this door."

Elena smiled.

"Thank you, Elena."

"Thank you, Celia. Good night."

"Good night," Celia replied, gently closing the door. Elena didn't hear another peep. She had wanted to add 'I love you' but decided, it was probably not a good idea.

The next morning, Elena was downstairs, packed, chi-kung'd and ready to go by 7. It seemed the couple who ran the place had been up a while. The husband greeted her as he sliced ham at the end of a long pine table made up for guests. The red-cheeked lady of the house served coffee in a bowl with a chunk of cheese, grapes, bread and boiled eggs. After topping up the caffeine, she placed next to Elena a packet of food wrapped in paper and tied with a string. She pointed a thick finger in the direction of the mountain.

"Good day! Pas de'pluie, pas du'vent!"

"Oui! Tres contente! Merci beaucoup pour le petit dej et la pique nique!"

The innkeeper nodded, grinned at her husband, and returned to her chores. Elena pulled out her phone and checked logistics. She reviewed the weather, the details of the route and changes in altitude. She added a large cushion to the normal expected hiking time. Ben's warnings had flashed in her mind more than once. With her inexperience, and without hiking boots, or company, she knew she had to take great care. She had slept well, and her body was itching to move. It seemed her legs were even more excited than she was.

At checkout, the landlady made her note down her route and destination, and checked her up and down, looking twice at her runners. She looked into Elena's eyes, smiled, and pointed to an exit at the end of a dark narrow corridor.

Outside, Elena was stopped by the glare and a rush of liveliness. She stood a few moments to adjust and take it all in.

The perfume was the freshness of a lush meadow. Beyond the cottage lay a field of illuminated grass. Above the green hills, shocking bleached-white curls of cloud suspended from a sky of sapphire blue.

There was no question as to which direction. There was one, well-trodden dirt and stone track, winding through flush pink wildflowers. In the distance, a monumental snow-capped mountain ridge, celestial in its beauty, towered towards the sky. Timeless and unyielding. Her heart was leaping.

Boy, I don't know what's real and what's not. Mamma! How can this be. There's angels dancing on my shoulders! Pas de'vent, pas de'pluie!

And off she went, almost at a skip, singing to herself, swinging her arms, up into the world of high mountains.

Many songs later, she saw another walker. It must still be off-season, she thought. A thin figure appeared around the bend further up, a silver-haired lady in hiking gear. As she neared, Elena could see the folds of bronze skin, the faded cloth, her sure footing and long stride. No creaking knees or hips on this madam of the mountain. Closer still and the woman's eyes were smiling and filled with light so striking that Elena could barely emit a Bonjour before she'd passed by. A small near empty daysack was visible on her back. Where exactly had she come from, Elena wondered. Eva Lodge was a day's walk. She called after her.

"Bonjour! Hello!"

The woman spun around in her hiking boots.

"Hello!" she said with an Irish accent.

"Have you walked from Eva?"

"Sure."

Elena decided against challenging this response.

"How's the path?"

"That depends."

"Right."

"No wind. No rain. With cat feet you'd be fine, mighty fine. Just keep goin'. You've plenty of time. Just keep singin'."

Before Elena could think of what to say she was off. An incessant whistling call shifted Elena's attention from the vanishing hiker to a riot of red kites circling above.

Soon after, the way became increasingly uneven, and she had to take greater care not to slip on the stones. Due to the higher altitude, the grass had gone. She had passed the treeline.

After walking through a narrow mountain pass, the view opened up and she could see the trail ahead wind around a mountain face capped with snow. She stopped for water and listened to her feet. As she rested, a pair of hikers from behind walked past, at speed, carrying metal sticks, nodding at her as they flew by. She wished that they had lingered a little. Was this the serious hiker greeting, she wondered, pleased to be among other walkers for a change. After adjusting the laces and the tightness of her rucksack, she set off.

As the way became steeper, she was forced to slow down. Labored breath and leg ache reminded her how unaccustomed she was to mountain hiking. She tried to concentrate on adapting her posture to the incline. She breathed more deeply and took her time. She thought about the mountain itself, its old age and seasons, its strength, the entire depth and shape of it. As she landed each step lightly, and moved her body in an even rhythm, she began to feel more connected to the world around her and absorbed by the experience. The sensation helped her to use less energy. After a minor slip on loose stones, she swiftly regained her step. Her centre of gravity had shifted. She crouched slightly lower, and stretched her legs in the stride.

Further on up the constant ascent, she was hit by a wave of fatigue. She had to stop. She rested against a ledge.

It's okay, she said to herself. It's okay to stop. It's normal.

She was surrounded by stones and rocks and a patchwork of moving cloud. Her rucksack felt heavier, her back damp with sweat. She checked her phone. There was no signal. Her battery was dying. That was quick, she thought, as fear crept in.

She had never hiked this high before. The distant view to one side, a green valley, was a struggle to appreciate. Rising anxiety had erased all traces of her earlier euphoria and she couldn't face it down. She knew she was ill-prepared for where she was, and the fear was justified. "May you serve me," she said out loud to the fear, "and keep me safe. Keep me alert, but *don't steal my energy*." She pulled out a seed bar and ate it without regard for its taste. It was fuel. She washed it down with a little water.

Startling her, by the side of the track, was a small dead bird, brown, with a rust-colored breast and a mottled pattern on its coat. A creature had picked at the corpse. She wondered what it was doing here, seemingly an inhospitable place for small brown birds.

As she rose, she felt the strain in her legs, glutes and back muscles, and fatigue everywhere. Her physical body wanted her to take off the rucksack and lie down. But at the pace she was going, she could not keep stopping to rest if she was to make the lodge by day's end. As she carried on, she noticed it was harder to breathe. She struggled on, slowly, and wondered why there were so few hikers.

By now, she had lost all interest in the scenery and her view narrowed. The track ahead. The track ahead. The hike was becoming a serious challenge and the sole objective now was to reach its end safely. But she *was* out of her depth. She thought of her Dad and pushed the thought away and tried instead to zero in on her step, but she felt so tired, and what was it, was it *anger* rising? Images of her father flashed in her mind, and she remembered the way he would sometimes speak to Mum, the jibes, the 'humor', the countless ways he would dismiss and exclude her, diminish her, set her aside, the constant belittling, subtle in his execution, sometimes not, but perfectly clear now to Elena, resonating through time. She had heard many speak like that to the most important person in their life.

Her father was a doctor, a specialist in repairing and replacing skin. She heard the beeps of his pager and remembered his constant disappearing and how her Mum fell apart when he left for good. She remembered herself curling in a ball on the dirt on the other side of the house with her hands over her ears. Through her tight hands, she could still hear her mother screaming as the police came and dragged her away.

Elena was about to burst into tears but felt a rising wave of anger. She looked around to be certain she was alone. She stooped down with her hands on her thighs, and in a torrent of abuse, let her rage crash onto the stone. When there was nothing left, she hung a moment, silent, and all she could hear was her hard breath, in and out. She turned and leaned and kept on up, climbing and listening to the crackling sound of her shoes against the loose stony ground. Exhausted, she thought of nothing for a while, just focusing on each foot against the earth. But the twist of fear was not far away, its rationale well-founded and unmoving, as if she was rowing a precarious boat on an unforgiving sea.

What am I doing here? How insane is this? A novice, walking solo, on a mountain. Wearing runners. How stupid. She felt a soft breeze against her face and shouted, "pas de fucking vent!" And the breeze cooled the heat at the back of her neck and she sighed and she laughed, and coughed, and was forced to stop until the coughing stopped and her breath was restored.

In the pause, she turned inwards and saw at once, a torrid of angry feelings, and remembered. Closing her eyes, she said *yes* to them all, penetrating the anger, witnessing the many times she herself had felt her own spirit dimmed by mockery, menace, loathing, exclusion, her voice gagged by custom and the powerful. She began muttering out loud '*mercy, merciful*'.

A softness of inner calm poured in and out from her chest, and as before, as she'd done before, she began to trace the countless ways she had experienced kindness and support. She started moving again and remembered how her father had tried to help her Mum, and why he had no choice but to take custody of young Freddie with her long spells in hospital and no end in sight. All those years, no contact with her Dad, until the funeral, but it was, indeed it was, so fine they were back in touch. He hadn't retired. He had never been much available, though she didn't make it easy either living 25 hours by plane. And hadn't she followed in his long shadow, long hospital shifts that consume your life, forever tied to the flow of patients. And they had both done good work and she felt proud, and she felt both distant and close to him. She loved the fact that it was *he* who had convinced the hospital and enabled her mum to follow her passion.

The erratic play of clouds had been consumed by a bank of darker grey. It had come out of nowhere.

"Oh mountain, what's next for me!" she cried out loud.

I said I am ready to learn. You took me at my word! Taking me, shaking me!

Silence, apart from the hollow of a haunting wind. Head down, she carried on. One step would get her closer, and another.

While you're at it, I need to know... what's next, the big next. What should I be doing with my days when this walk is done?

The cloud had started to wrap itself around the mountain and it was hard to see where the path was leading though it was starting to flatten out. She could still see ahead of her about 5-6 meters. The swift change in weather at high altitude rattled her, and as best she could, she quickened her pace. She thought of nothing now but of the way she was walking, and on and on she hiked, on through a small gorge to the next incline, across the mountain ridge, ignoring her fatigue, only thinking now how to optimize each step. She got the hang of grabbing her water bottle out from the side of her rucksack without stopping. She had begun to make some distance when the slope began to steepen again. While thanks to the smaller worn stones, the direction was clear, the clouds had invaded her immediate surroundings. Now, it was much harder to see ahead. Her leg muscles ached and made themselves heard. Thoughts of *enough!* flooded her mind. She stopped and shouted "ENOUGH!"

She listened for any noises and all she could hear was her labored breath. She closed her eyes. In her mind, in the distance, a blue dot of light appeared, gradually growing and coming closer, in the form of Petrus. He appeared radiant, his energy flowing through her, and just the thought of this, gave her a surge of power. As she scrambled up the incline, shifting her weight, she imagined she was full of the blue light and that she was a cat, moving like a panther. She made some progress.

The fog parted in patches. No longer did it hide just where she was. She looked down from the path, gasping.

Inches from her feet, was a sheer drop, to the hillside edge of the valley below. Heart pounding, an image filled her mind of her slipping and falling to her death. She shook her head and willed herself to a heightened state of strength and awareness.

It worked, for a time. The pain in her legs was escorted off-stage and pulled to the back row. She pushed forward steadily, with great care, and thinking of nothing else. After a turn in the trail, she stopped and glanced to the side. Whilst the drop was still very steep, the sheer cliff had gone. But the moment's pause broke her concentration. Her fatigue returned with a vengeance. It was affecting her balance and alertness. Her mind cloudy, she wiped the sweat dripping into her eyes. Thinking she should rest, just a moment, she paused, and pulled off her rucksack. The sudden relief of losing weight brought a rush of light-headedness. She checked the time on her fading phone. It was the first thing to slip from her hands.

She had failed to detect the stones beneath her feet were loose. As she lent down to pick up her phone, the path seemed to fall away. In an instant, before she could grab onto safety, she had lost her footing, and was gone. She disappeared from the track.

Tumbling down the steep, angular slope, she skidded on her back, thumping the side of the mountain. Terrified, she threw herself around to grip onto the rocky surface, grasping at lumps of stone. They fell away in her hand. She felt her body sliding faster. As she grappled to cling to the mountain, time stopped. She saw herself, then and there, falling to her death. In that moment, she realized, she wasn't scared. She felt instead, a feeling of infinite love. But in the next moment, a mighty urge *to live* rushed into her being. One rock didn't move, and another, and she scrambled and scratched a place for a secure hold. Breathing hard and fast, she managed to halt her fall. She could hear stones skipping down beneath her, skirting off the mountain side and into the depths below. But she felt strong, eerily strong, animal strong.

In one iron heave, she lunged up the face, finding a hold, and another, each time, securing her hands and feet like a vice. She made her way, steady, all the way back up, one grasp at a time. As the incline eased, she was able to clamber up on all fours and onto the track, and back to the rest of her life.

She sat slumped, her legs splayed on the ground. Her heart was a hammer. She was dizzy. She was in shock.

A wave rose up her chest ready to release a river of tears. At the same time, like a dam wall, a far stronger compulsion blocked the torrent – the urge to get up and get to safety. Daylight's end was near. Alone, where she was, in her state, to even think about what just happened, would be a luxury she could ill afford. She had no time to rest, think, feel or understand. Gripped by an automatic urgency, she tightened her shoes and gradually pulled herself up.

Standing, she paused to check her balance. She secured her phone, donned her pack, and with slow, deliberate steps, she carried on up into the cloud, her heart still beating to the edges of her being. After a while, she found some kind of stride, returning, with her heart, to a steady rhythm. Maintaining concentration, she was back in a flow, detached from the pain and fatigue. It felt now, as if she had entered another plane, expanding into the nature around her. She was moving but her sense of self became irrelevant, immaterial.

Finally, the ground flattened out and she caught sight of the most beautiful hiking sign she had ever seen. Attached to its base was a board for Eva Lodge. Close now. Safety. She could believe it. She stopped, dropped the rucksack and drained the rest of the water. It tasted insanely cool, fresh and clean. She could feel a welcome party in her body. She sat on the ground, leaned her back against the rockface and closed her eyes.

Like the hit of an anesthetic, a heaviness swept through her body. Tears of exhaustion streamed down her face. She let the emotion flow through her. Her breath gradually began to slow.

Oh my, oh my. Life's precious thread in the nearness of... I nearly fell. I nearly died. How was I able to climb back up? I am *not* that strong. Arms, hands, Petrus. Respect. Powerful Earth beneath my bones. At your mercy. To all life, to all love, beyond my understanding, with every cell, I give thanks. Her breathing deepened. She felt a tender embrace of a loving presence, and a fleeting sense the same energy was part of her future. She opened her eyes and looked at the ground beneath and around her and the clouds above. Everything was in sharp focus. The mountain felt alive. She felt a sense of endlessness. Her mind drifted. She thought of the Alps as they looked from the sky and all the mountains and lakes and oceans and the universe of stars and back again. She stood in the middle of a great plain and could hear her breath and the breath of all the people in the world, breathing in and out, in and out. She thought of all the creatures, all the living things from the elephant to the towering trees to the microbe. And she was with them. She was in them. And the breeze touched her face, and back she was. Eyes squinting. The weather had changed again. The bank of cloud was white.

The grip of fear and tension within her had gone, and in its release, she realized just how terrified she had been. She felt a deep ease. She spread her hands in the dirt. Her mother's ring had gone. The momentary regret passed and left her smiling, a smile somehow of herself as a child and her mother as a child and her mother and on. She sensed the birth of a certain confidence, a more rooted intuitive knowing, in the present moment. She knew, then and there, that the path beyond her travels would become clear, day by day, moment by moment, and she could face her future challenges with a strong and honest heart.

After a short stretch of undulating path, the angle stayed in a steady, moderate descent and while her legs ached, she felt joy. She knew where she was on the trail and that the lodge was nearby. She stopped to adjust her shoes. She took extra care where she placed her weary feet. There was only one way she wanted to descend. The clouds began to disperse, and she could see the trail winding ahead through a field. At the sight of the grass, she knew her safety was assured.

She found a spot for a sensational pee. Buttoned up, she thought of the food packet. A flattish rock became her seat.

The ham was sweet and the bread soft with a thick crust. The apple was a little sour and tasted amazing. She tidied away and was about to crack on when something made her stay. Next to the rock where she sat, the grass reached her fingertips.

Strange life, *how* did I pull myself up that cliff? When it mattered, I was strong, I was really strong! And what did I feel at the edge of life... and back there, resting on the mountain. Yes. *It was love.* Pure edgeless love. Not the love of a family, or a partner, though they were part of it, but a universal energy of love, that seems to connect us all, that is part of everything. This is my future. This is my present. When I thought I would die, it was love that mattered, in all its immensity, potentiality, gentleness and revelation. This is life, if I am true, to live and breathe and be, in this luminous sea.

She felt quiet and strong and a wide peace. As she rested, the clouds continued to clear, and there, revealed ahead of her, between two snow-capped mountain ranges, was a great river valley. The late sun reflected on the river as it wound between purple lowlands. The majesty swelled her heart and filled her eyes with tears of joy.

The mountain lodge, more like a large chalet-style budget

hotel, was lively with local hikers from every direction, and tourists who had taken the cable car from the valley below. Friends drinking beer, couples and families filled the self-serve restaurant of mostly long plank tables. It was a relaxed and fun atmosphere, but Elena could barely speak. At the reception counter, she struggled to explain her reservation and was grateful her passport could tell the story. She learned, from the anxious girl handing her a first aid case and pointing to the salle de bains, that her face was cut and she had blood on her shirt. A check in the bathroom mirror revealed superficial grazing and a rip in her sports bra. Her shirt off, she splashed her face and the front of her torso. A young man walked in carrying a small bag. She looked at him squarely and pointed at the damsel on the door.

"Pardon!" he quipped as he closed the door behind him and opened it again, a few seconds later.

"Are you okay? Je suis médecin, un étudiant en médecine. The hotel asked me to come."

She nodded to indicate she was fine.

"Have you seen your back?"

She twisted her body in the mirror and could see some blood between the shoulder blades. She picked up her shirt and saw the red rip in the back panel.

"Pardon," he said again. He washed his hands, took gloves and saline from the first aid case, and took a closer look. "It just needs a clean."

He washed and dressed the wounds as Elena leaned on the sink in silence.

"What's your name?" he asked.

"Elena. And yours?"

"Mathieu Rivoli. You've been climbing?"

"I guess you'd call it that."

"Alone?"

"Thank you for your kindness. I just need a meal and a sleep." He picked up her blood-stained shirt and held it open for her.

"You're welcome to join us if you like. We're in the restaurant."

"Merci beaucoup, Mathieu."

"Take care."

She sat in the quietest corner and relished a plate of sauerkraut and sausages. The barman brought her a glass of red wine she had not ordered.

"Are you Elena Lees?"

She looked up, perplexed.

He smiled and bowed his head slightly.

"From L'Auberge René."

"Oh! What an awesome lady," Elena said, thanking the waiter.

Sipping her wine, she noticed the junior doctor, at the other end of the room, ensconced with a group of friends some time past their first beer. The view through the thick windows was distant and dying in the light. She was glad for her earlier private panorama. She had absorbed the peace.

Delighted to shut the door to her own room, she collapsed on the bed, pulling off her shoes with her feet. As she sunk into sleep, she could hear the calling of red kites.

In her dreams, she was on a river, in a wood-paneled

boat, with colored cushions, soft rugs and lanterns. Her fellow passengers were there and not there. Beyond the boat it was a dark endless night without stars. She heard talking, and saw children walking along the water's edge, a familiar face, a boy with clean shoes, and then another, younger, neither boy nor girl, with bare-threaded clothes and broken feet. In the distance, a great city was on fire and thousands of hungry worn people, poured into the countryside. The fields turned into wheat and grass, and it was no longer night and sun wincing and trees and wildlife and wildflowers, and the banks were lush, the water clear. A group were walking nearby, but they were not people of today. Filled with light, gentle, moving with an ease and readiness, a woman turned to look at her and it seemed from her eyes, everything was understood. Elena saw at once that all of these people, were love, in a human form. Some of them knew what was in each other's minds, and the woman could see into Elena, who she was, and her mother and father, and all her ancestors all the way back, and at the same time, so too could Elena. The woman turned to a young man, a familiar face, and he held up his arm and a bridge of light appeared and reached her boat. He was waving and he called out to her to come but he was calling *Petrus! Petrus!*

Elena woke, her eyes wide, looking straight ahead towards the ceiling and the hut dropped away and the world dropped away. She felt an expanding ball of energy in the palm of both hands. She stood and walked to the thick window and opened the latch to the dawn. Lifting the sky, she slowly raised her arms up and back down to her side and stood still. Her feet steady, her body swayed like a willow and returned to stillness. She looked in the direction of the view a long while. She closed her eyes, and in her mind and body and heart, she was as free as a young child, and alight in an ocean of light and the revelation of love. She posed the question, *next?* But already she knew.

daviesWriter.com

Acknowledgements

May I take this chance to express my gratitude to the many people who have supported me in the writing of this book, with special thanks to Fred Leebron for his unstinting encouragement and inspiring notes, and to Scott Collins and Elizabeth Foster for their constant support.

The manuscript benefited from the expert scrutiny of Andrea Walker, Anastasia Parkes, Caroline Leavitt and Bridget Lane, and I am grateful for the inspirational support of many, including Gabriel Griffin and the Lake Orta Festival Poets, Cathy Smith Bowers, Rev David Wallace, Ian Davies, B.C. Wilson, Lourdes Holtzhauer, Nicolas Rabeau, Stella Koupadi, Marci Shimoff, Deborah Distefano, Kim Forcina, Rev Jean Marie Harper, Elissa Shore, Cari Jo Melgoza-Garcia, Cheri Saundry, Meta Mehling, Elizabeth Baughan, Chris Foster, Morella Hibon, Glen Matthews, Kathryn Giblin, Nathanaël Chouraqui, Blandine Sixdenier, Dominykas Broga and Sinan Al Hawat.

In addition, I would like to extend special thanks to Jonathan Star for his kindness in granting me permission to quote from his translation of the Tao Te Ching (J P Tarcher-Penguin 2001).

May I also take this opportunity to express my deep appreciation for the inspiriting support of my sons, Alex and Jean Rabeau, to whom the book is dedicated.

Printed in Great Britain
by Amazon

c1599ce4-11cb-4fa8-87c5-39c1e997971aR01